TATE

VAULT

›

Tate James
VAULT: Madison Kate Novella
Copyright © Tate James 2021
All rights reserved
First published in 2021
James, Tate
Vault: Madison Kate Novella

Cover design: Stephanie Heinritz
Editing: Heather Long (content) and Jax Garren (line).

To everyone who cursed my name and got the angry eye twitches when I pretended this novella didn't exist.

We all know that wasn't a typo.

WANT TO CHAT ABOUT BOOKS WITH TATE?

Facebook: shorturl.at/qstN6

Readers Group: shorturl.at/npv01

Twitter: shorturl.at/prvO3

Pinterest: shorturl.at/qI135

Instagram: shorturl.at/exzN6

Stay up to date with Tate James by signing up for her mailing
list:

http://eepurl.com/dfFR5v

Website: https://www.tatejamesauthor.com

MADISON KATE
NOVELLA

TATE JAMES

DISCLAIMER

Vault is a Madison Kate Novella but is intended to be read *after* the Hades series as several events overlap and this story DOES contain multiple spoilers for the Hades series. Please consult the recommended reading order for Shadow Grove World on my website if you are uncertain what order to read the books in. This novella is set on a timeline parallel to the events of *Club 22* and *Timber*.

Once again. This story **WILL** spoil the Hades series for you if you haven't read or finished it prior to picking this up.

You've been warned.

MADISON KATE

Early morning sunlight sparkled over the pool, and I yawned into my measly, normal-person-sized coffee. We'd only been at this safe house a couple of days, but I had yet to find a coffee mug bigger than eleven ounces and Steele had given me a hard look when I'd pondered filling up a flower pot. Not that I actually would have... It had holes in the bottom.

"This fucking sucks." My pale, red-haired friend sulked from underneath a wide umbrella. Even first thing in the morning, she was cautious not to get sunburned.

"Drinking coffee by the pool of an Italian villa?" Kody asked, his fingertips trailing down my bare arm. He was seated behind me on the sun lounger, my body snuggled between his legs and his chest against my back. "I dunno, there're worse places to be."

Seph lowered her sunglasses to shoot him a glare. "You *know* what I mean, dickhead. This whole Italian *vacation* is total bullshit. Dare is being massively overprotective—like, worse than usual. I think she might have finally lost the plot." She mumbled the last part, and none of us believed she meant it. Not even her.

I tipped my head back to give Kody a hard look, but he just shook his head in return. No, I wasn't permitted to fill my friend in on all the dark, depraved things that had happened to her family. It wasn't my place, and Seph's sister—the infamous and downright terrifying Hades—wouldn't appreciate it.

I huffed a frustrated sigh and pushed up from my comfy position on Kody's chest. "I feel you, girl," I sympathized instead of saying what I really wanted to: That we'd moved from her aunt's vineyard in Tuscany after multiple remote explosive devices had been found planted around the house. That her sister wasn't being *over*protective... just plain protective. I didn't blame her.

"Come on, let's get wet before the sun rises enough that you hibernate indoors," I teased, stripping my sundress off since I already had a bikini on underneath.

Seph shot me a sly smile. "Oh, like you haven't been *wet* enough this morning."

My cheeks heated instantly, and I shot Kody an accusing

glare. "So much for being quiet."

He just grinned and finished off my coffee, which I'd left beside the sun lounge. "I said quiet*er,* as in you didn't deafen *all* the neighbors this time."

I had no good comebacks for that. In my defense, though, I wouldn't be such a screamer if the sex wasn't so goddamn incredible. The way his gaze heated as I met his eyes said he knew it and wasn't the slightest bit sorry.

"Guys, *quit it,*" Seph complained, standing up to pull her own sundress off. "You're doing that eye-fucking thing again, and it's making me uncomfortable as shit."

Not giving me a chance to eye-fuck Kody anymore, she shoved me hard, and I flew backward into the pool with a laugh. She followed me a split second later, showing me her middle finger under the water before we both surfaced.

For a while we just played around in the pool while Kody dozed in the early morning sunlight, but I knew Seph was itching to get out of the house. She'd been protected and sheltered her whole life, but now that she was *aware* of it, she was going stir-crazy.

"Hey, why don't we head down into Sorrento for brunch," I suggested after we climbed out. I grabbed a couple of towels and tossed her one. Kody had already gone inside, so I probably should go and run it past the guys first. But whatever. "We could go shopping and have pizza…"

Seph wrinkled her nose. "Pizza for breakfast?"

I shrugged. "Brunch, but whatever. When in Rome."

"We're not in Rome," she shot back, but she was grinning. I was confident she was on board with my idea.

"Semantics," I replied with an eye roll. "Go shower and change; I'll work on getting the guys to agree."

Seph groaned dramatically. "I'll be sure to wear my earplugs and make it a long shower in that case."

Snickering, I followed her into the house. "You wanna go to town or not? Because they're not just going to *agree* without a little persuasion." Especially not after the bomb scare in Tuscany.

"You're an addict, MK," Seph told me with a smile. "But yes, I want to go shopping and eat pizza for breakfast, so... go work that magical pussy energy."

"Brunch," I corrected as she hurried upstairs to her bedroom and attached bathroom.

I made my way through the huge villa to the rooms I was sharing with my guys and found Steele still sprawled out in bed, reading something on his tablet. Archer was on the phone, pacing the room with a pair of low-slung sweats *barely* holding onto the curve of his ass and no shirt on.

Steele looked up when I headed across the room and tossed his tablet aside. "Hellcat," he greeted me with a smile. "You're all wet."

I licked my lips and shot him a suggestive look. "Around you?

Always. But I just suggested to Seph that we all head down to Sorrento for shopping and brunch—"

"No," Archer snapped, still in the middle of his call but answering my yet unasked question.

I cocked one brow at him, then turned back to Steele. "As I was saying, before being so rudely interrupted, Seph is going nuts being cooped up all the time. It might be nice to—"

"I said *no*," Archer barked again, then scowled. "No, not you, Rich. Sorry, I was talking to Kate. Yeah, continue."

Steele and I both gave him a long look. Then I shot Steele a smirk. "Max, baby. You don't let Sunshine call the shots, do you?"

His smile was slow and lazy. "Nice try, Hellcat. What's in it for me to side with you against Arch?"

"Blow job?" I suggested, grinning.

Steele barked a laugh. "Sold." He crossed his ink-covered arms behind his head, his tongue stud flashing as he smiled at me.

I wasn't messing around. He was only in a pair of boxers, so I tugged them down and palmed his rising cock as I licked my lips. "Good deal," I murmured, stroking him harder, "shopping and brunch in Sorrento."

Steele's response was a sharp inhale as I dipped down to swirl my tongue around his tip.

"What the fuck?" Archer exclaimed.

I tipped my face to throw him a smirk, then licked my way down every one of Steele's eight piercings lining the underside of his dick.

"No, *Christ!* Not you, Rich," Archer snarled into the phone again, his knuckles turning white with how hard he was gripping it. "Can I call you back?"

I chuckled softly, then filled my mouth with Steele's dick. My tongue flicked each of those piercings as I took him deeper, and his hands went to my hair.

"Surely this isn't *that* important," Archer was growling to his manager on the phone. "I can call back in half an hour." Pause. Curse. "Fine. Yes, *yes*, I get it. Fine, carry on."

"Oh shit," Steele groaned as I sucked his length. "Fuck, Hellcat." His fingers wove tighter in my hair, his hips bucking up to slam deeper into my throat. My damp towel slipped off my body, and I wiggled my ass teasingly in Archer's general direction. Now that I thought about it, he had mentioned an important call with his manager this morning.

"Well, well, this is a nice surprise," Kody purred, strutting out of the bathroom with a cloud of steam billowing behind him.

"Fuck you, don't you fucking dare," Archer snapped, stalking over to the window seat to slouch against the glass with his phone still at his ear. "Not *you*, Rich. Kody. He's being a prick."

Kody just grinned. "If I was being a prick... I'd probably do something like *this*." Humming a happy tune, he circled around to the foot of the bed, then tugged the ties of my bikini bottoms open. The wet swimsuit dropped uselessly to the bed, and Kody gave a snicker of pure evil as he did the same to my top.

"Hellcat wants to take Seph into Sorrento for shopping and brunch," Steele informed Kody with a short groan as I sucked him deep again. "Arch said no."

Kody grabbed my ass cheeks with both hands. "I fucking love brunch." A split second later his tongue was inside me, and I almost choked on Steele's dick.

I pulled back a moment to catch my breath, and Kody took that as encouragement to bury his face deeper between my legs, his lips finding my clit. Archer just glared *death* at the three of us, which, really, he should know only made us act up worse.

Steele bucked his hips, reminding me I was in the middle of something. So I broke eye contact with Archer and went back to business, stroking and sucking Steele's dick.

"Arch still talking with Rich about that fight in Monaco?" Kody asked, surfacing for air and replacing his tongue with his fingers.

Steele grunted a sound of confirmation, his hands pushing my head down on his metal studded cock.

Kody gave a low chuckle. "Too bad, bro." He shifted to his knees, then gripped my hips as he pushed his thick cock into my pussy.

I moaned around Steele's girth, shudders of intense arousal rippling through me.

"Keep it *quiet* this time, babe." Kody chuckled, pushing in further as I rocked back against him. "I don't need another lecture from Demi."

"No, *Rich*," Archer snapped to his phone, "clearly I wasn't listening. Repeat the question."

I glanced over, my mouth still full of dick, and watched as he shoved his hand inside his sweatpants to take care of the tent he was pitching. He met my eyes and gave a slow shake of his head like he was silently trying to warn me not to keep messing with him.

Idiot. That was just waving a red flag at a bull.

I rocked harder onto Kody's dick and hollowed my cheeks as I sucked Steele, my elbows holding my balance on the mattress. Kody didn't need any further encouragement, though, gripping my hips and pumping into me with whispered curses on his lips.

Steele pushed my head down harder, his hips bucking faster as he fucked my mouth, and I squeezed the base of his shaft with my fingers to hold him steady. He was so close already; I could feel it in the way his cock throbbed and swelled against my tongue.

"Make her come while she's still gagged," Steele ordered Kody, his breathing rough.

Kody huffed a laugh. "Good thinking." His hand slipped around to find my clit, and his fingers rubbed it with quick, well-practiced circles as he fucked me harder and harder until—

"Shit," Steele exhaled as I moaned and thrashed, bucking my hips as I came. "Yep, that'll do it." His dick thickened, and he pushed deeper as he came, pulsing his seed right into my throat. I swallowed on reflex, drinking him down and still moaning with my own climax lingering.

Kody grunted, his fingers digging into my flesh as he fucked me hard enough that Archer's manager *surely* heard the slapping of skin on skin. Then he found his own release inside me, gasping and cursing as his cock jerked.

When he released me, I pushed myself up on shaking arms, then wobbled over to the window seat where Archer still had his hand inside his pants and his phone to his ear. Not that he'd probably heard a word that had been said.

Biting my lip, I sank to my knees and tilted my head in question.

He held my gaze, his lids heavy and his breathing harsh. When I didn't move, he gave a long exhale.

"Fine," he muttered. "Brunch, no shopping."

Grinning my victory, I peeled his sweatpants down and used my mouth to finish the job his hand had started. What had Seph called me, again? Addicted? Yeah, no denying that. I was a certifiable dick-addict. But only for these three... my true loves.

2

STEELE

As badly as I wanted to watch my girl as she skipped along the cobblestone street, arm in arm with her friend, I had to stay alert. We'd been hired to do a job, not take a vacation, and the recent discovery of bombs around Demi's vineyard had given us the reminder we needed. Seph was still in danger, and if we let anything happen to her on our watch... well then, it'd be the three of us in danger.

"This is a bad idea," Archer muttered beside me, his sharp gaze scanning our surroundings. His hand was under his loose jacket, probably resting on the butt of his gun.

I gave a small shrug. "Probably, but you agreed, so quit

your bitching."

He shot me a salty glare. "Under duress."

Kody and I both snickered at that.

"Oh yeah, you *hated* that persuasion," Kody teased. "We could tell."

Arch had nothing to say back to that, so he just flipped us a middle finger and moved to catch up with Demi and her wife, Stacey. Stacey was the only one of us who spoke fluent Italian, so she was playing the role of translator and tour guide when we ventured out into public spaces.

"As if he wouldn't have agreed if she'd just batted her lashes and called him Sunshine," Kody muttered to me with a chuckle as we made our way inside the restaurant the girls had chosen. "Under duress, my ass."

I smirked my agreement, my gaze moving over every patron inside the restaurant. The odds of Chase Lockhart having one of his goons planted in the randomly selected restaurant that we'd had no plans of visiting were low. But it never hurt to be vigilant.

Archer, big protective bastard that he was, tried to maneuver MK into the most protected seat at our table, but she just shoved him and put Seph there instead—as it should be when Seph was the one in danger. Still, I got where Arch was coming from. My own natural instinct was to protect MK over *anyone* else too.

While he was busy engaging in a silent argument with her via intense eye contact, I slid into the seat directly beside her.

The one Archer had his hand on the back of like he'd been about to sit there.

"You snooze, you lose, D'Ath," I told him, stretching my arm out around MK's shoulders and getting comfy.

Seph wrinkled her nose as she eyed us. "The fact that you guys are still fighting over who gets to sit next to your girlfriend is equally adorable and nauseating."

My Hellcat just gave me a warm smile, leaned into my embrace, and smacked a kiss on my cheek. Meanwhile, Archer huffed and sank down into the seat beside me.

"Wife," he muttered. "She's *my* wife."

Seph rolled her eyes. "Don't start with me on *that*."

"I still have those divorce papers if you ever need them, MK," Demi offered from further down the table, a mischievous smirk on her lips.

Archer looked downright murderous at that, though. MK was tuned into his moods enough that she'd sensed it just as easily as Kody and I had, and she simply smiled as she inspected the heirloom D'Ath ring on her finger.

"Nah, I think I'll keep him," she replied, shooting Archer a heated look. "He does this thing with his tongue—"

"Stop!" Seph exclaimed. "We know. Change the damn subject."

My girl laughed but obliged her friend and shifted the conversation to school—seeing as Seph was trying to maintain her classes via online learning while we were out of the country.

Despite the casual chat between the women at the table, Kody, Arch, and I stayed alert and tense, prepared for anything. It wasn't until we'd almost finished our mouthwatering, wood-fired pizzas that MK cajoled us into relaxing a bit.

When Kody joined them on the next round of cocktails, Archer muttered something under his breath about doing a sweep of the perimeter and stalked away from the table.

MK watched him go, then when he disappeared from sight, she shifted her gaze to me with concern etched across her face. "Is it just me," she murmured, "or is he in a mood?"

I winced. She hadn't known Arch a fraction of the time Kody and I had, but she read his body signals almost better than both of us now. "Not just you. I think he's taking it personally that he didn't spot those explosive devices."

Her frown deepened. "Aren't we all?"

I flashed her a quick smile, then gave Kody a nod. "Go check on him; make sure he's not harassing some innocent tourist who looked slightly suspicious."

Kody scoffed but clearly thought it was a possibility because he went to do as I'd asked without argument. The whole bomb threat situation had us all on edge, but it'd reinforced how serious our task was—not just keeping Seph safe on Hades's orders but also protecting MK. She so frequently hung out with her bubbly friend that it'd be damn easy for her to get caught in the crossfire.

I dropped my hand to her knee, pulling her slightly closer as my own protectiveness reared its head inside my mind.

"You keep grabbing me like that, and I drag you into the bathroom here," MK whispered with a flirty glance. Seph was engaged in conversation with Demi and Stacey, none of them paying attention to the two of us. Would they notice if we slipped away?

Dammit. I *just* sent Kody away from the table.

"I don't know about that, Hellcat," I murmured back, my fingers creeping up her thigh. Whoever the hell had invented the flirty little sundresses she'd been wearing since we arrived in Italy needed a goddamn high five. Talk about easy access. "These tablecloths are long enough..." My fingers danced higher, and her breath caught.

Fuck, I loved that sound. That tiny, excited gasp that she made when she was turned on.

"Max..." Okay, I changed my mind. I loved *that* sound more. The way she half sighed, half moaned my name... holy *fuck*, it got me hard.

"Hellcat," I replied, dragging my teeth over my lip as she slouched in her chair, practically begging me to take things further right there at the table across from Seph's aunts. Shit, I didn't need any convincing and gave zero fucks if they knew what we were doing. So I moved my hand higher and hooked a finger under the edge of her already damp panties.

I hoped like hell we never left this honeymoon phase where

we could hardly keep our hands off each other. It was my perfect definition of a happily ever after.

A breathy gasp escaped her parted lips, and she instantly remembered we were in public. *Dammit*. Her thighs snapped closed, trapping my hand as she reached for her drink in an effort to regain her composure.

"You two okay over there?" Stacey asked us with a knowing smile.

"Fine!" MK replied in a slightly strangled voice. She'd trapped my hand, and I wasn't wasting the opportunity. As she took a gulp of her drink, I pushed a finger inside her hot, tight cunt, and she spluttered, "Just... um, talking about... things. Stuff. Ignore us."

Stacey grinned, shaking her head. "Will do. Carry on." She very deliberately shifted her chair so that she was facing her wife and gave us her shoulder.

I took her at her command and added a second finger.

MK squirmed and glared at me hard. She didn't push me away, though. "Max, what are you—" Her question broke off with a soft moan as my thumb found her clit beneath the table. "Shit."

"Shh," I whispered with a laugh. "Act natural. Tell me about what's going on with your company. You had an update from Monica last night, didn't you?"

Her eyes bugged out like she couldn't believe I had the audacity to ask about business while fingering her cunt in a restaurant. But really, she couldn't be *that* shocked. It sure as fuck wasn't the first time we'd been too impatient to find total privacy.

"Um, yeah," she replied, and it sounded all kinds of sexy with an echo of a moan as my thumb danced across her swollen clit and my fingers stroked her tight pussy's walls. "Yeah, she didn't really have anything new to update me on. Except it sounded like—*ah fuck*—like, um, like..."

I grinned when she trailed off, her gaze going unfocused as I pressed my thumb down hard on her clit. "Like what, Hellcat?"

"Like I should teach you a fucking lesson by going to jump Archer's bones right now," she muttered back, but the way her hips rocked against my hand told a different story. Holy shit, I was addicted to this girl. She was utterly perfect in every way that mattered to me.

I can't wait to marry her.

Dragging my tongue over my lip, I moved my fingers faster, watching her face intently, searching for the subtle cues that she was about to come.

"Shit, Steele," she hissed, her napkin balled in her fist on the tabletop. Then something across the restaurant seemed to catch her attention, and not in a good way. Her whole body stiffened, and her gaze sharpened.

"What is it?" I demanded. In a flash my hand was out of her panties and on the butt of my gun as I whipped my face around to look for whatever had startled her.

"Seph, get down!" MK yelled, launching herself out of her

seat a split second before the waiter I'd just spotted threw a knife our way.

Everything happened in slow motion. Hellcat shoved Seph, the thrown knife blurred past my face, then my girl gave a scream of pain that made me see *red*. Blood red.

3

KODY

We'd seen Archer's mood rapidly declining for the last week or so... but that swipe Demi had taken about MK divorcing him had tipped him dangerously close to the breaking point. He was taking our assigned task—protecting Seph—crazy serious. We all were. But we'd also had numerous hypothetical discussions around what would happen if it came to protecting MK over Seph. The bomb scare had made us reconsider things.

Seph was great, no doubt. She was a nice girl—if sheltered and spoiled as hell—and had been a loyal friend to MK. But she wasn't our soulmate. She was never going to be our number one priority, and the no-longer-hypothetical *what-if* of finding those explosives was pushing the issue.

"We can't keep doing this," Archer snapped, pacing the cobblestones outside the restaurant. He was eyeing every person entering the restaurant with suspicion. "Sooner or later, Kate's going to get hurt. Besides, don't we have our own lives to get on with? How long are we supposed to play babysitter?"

I shrugged. "As long as it fucking takes, bro. Or do *you* want to tell Hades that we can't be bothered to protect her little sister anymore? Remember what happened last time someone threatened Seph's safety?" Like I needed to bring that up. The Timberwolf massacre night, the *Lockhart* massacre, had been a pivotal point in all our lives. In most ways, Archer, Steele, and I had benefited greatly from that night. But we'd also seen firsthand what Hades would do to protect the ones she loved.

Archer scowled at me, then exhaled heavily. "Fuck," he groaned, rubbing his hand over his short beard. "Fair point. Then let's find somewhere *totally* isolated. This is way too public."

"Agreed," I replied, nodding. "Any one of these hundreds of strangers could be—"

A familiar, feminine scream cut me off, followed by three gunshots. Chaos erupted from the restaurant, and my blood ran cold. Archer reacted a fraction faster than me, shoving panicked patrons aside as he raced back into the restaurant with me tight on his heels.

The scene in front of us slammed home, confirming *all* our fears at once. Steele with his gun in hand, a waiter dead on the floor in a puddle of blood, and our girl—our fucking *heart*—soaked in blood and groaning in pain.

"Kate!" Archer exclaimed, rushing toward her. She held a hand up sharply to stop him, though, scowling.

"Get Seph to safety!" she snarled at him. "It's just a fucking flesh wound."

Flesh wound. Funny girl. There was a *knife sticking out of her goddamn shoulder*.

Archer seemed frozen in pained indecision, but Demi was already hauling Seph up from the floor and shoving the pale girl at him, providing the direction he needed.

"I've got her," I told him, jerking my head over my shoulder. He needed to get Seph to our car, and we needed to get the hell out of town.

Archer's face was pure thunder, but he wrapped his hand around Seph's arm and dragged her out of the restaurant after him, gun in his other hand as he totally ignored her protests.

"Babe," I exclaimed, scooping MK up off the ground but being careful not to bump the knife. We could pull it out back at the house where we could patch her up properly, and it might serve as evidence if we needed it.

"Kody, fucking hell, there's nothing wrong with my legs," she snarled, but I just shook my head as I carried her out. Steele exchanged a few words with Demi and Stacey, dropped a thick wad of money onto the table, then hurried to catch up with us.

He said something about Stacey handling the police, but I wasn't paying attention. My sole focus was on the way MK's face was creased in pain and the vibrant scarlet of her blood staining her tanned arm. Fuck. *Fuck*. If that bastard'd had better aim...

It'd been too close. Too fucking close.

"Kody," she snapped, pinching my arm to get my attention. "I'm *fine*. You can put me down."

I was still racing toward where we'd left our cars and didn't even slow at her suggestion, just shook my head. Words were too fucking hard with how much pure *fear* was running through me. She was bleeding. I'd sworn I'd never let her get hurt again, and here we were...

"Let's go," Steele barked as we climbed into the van. Archer was behind the wheel already, and Seph was sitting in the passenger seat with wide, glassy eyes. She was in shock, no question about it, but the three of us couldn't give two shits. *She* wasn't the one with a knife sticking out of her flesh. *She* wasn't the girl we'd burn the whole world down to protect, no matter how indebted to Hades we might be.

Seph knew it, too. I'd never met someone who wanted to be protected *less* than Persephone Timber. Ignorance would do that to a person, though.

"Demi and Stace?" Archer barked, and Steele shook his head.

"They'll meet us back at the house. Stacey needs to handle the cops and grease the right hands to clean up the scene, and Demi won't leave her to do it alone." He reached over both me and MK and gently fastened our seatbelt without bumping her arm.

I wasn't willing to let her go to sit on her own, so I gave him a small nod of thanks.

Archer glanced in the mirror, waiting until we were belted in before hitting the gas and tearing out of our parking spot. It was only a ten-minute drive up to the villa we had rented in this sleepy village, but the way Archer drove meant we got back in about half of that. Every bump and corner had MK gritting her teeth in pain, though, and by the time we stopped, I wanted to deck Archer myself for reckless driving.

"Give her to me," Archer snapped, throwing the door open before we could even release our seat belts.

"I'm not a dog," she snapped. "And I'm not dead. Jesus fucking Christ, you need to go and cool off, D'Ath; I'm not in the mood for the alpha-male bullshit routine."

I reluctantly released her as she wriggled free of my lap, but Archer wasn't budging when she tried to push past him. Instead, he swept her up in his arms like I'd just been holding her and stalked into the house while she hurled insults at him.

"You guys," a small voice jerked my attention away from Arch and MK. "I'm so sorry. This is all my fault."

Seph looked like she was on the verge of tears, her lower lip wobbling and her eyes all watery. Shit. Crying girls were not my thing at *all*.

"Not your fault," I muttered when Steele said fucking *nothing*. Thanks a lot, asshole. "Shit like that is what we're here for. To keep *you* safe. MK takes that task just as seriously as the rest of us."

"Let's get inside," Steele mumbled. "We need to pack up and sort out a new safe house. Clearly this location is compromised."

Seph's big eyes darted between the both of us, then she gave a small nod. "Okay. Sure. Is MK going to be okay, though?"

She'd better be.

"Yeah, it might just be a couple of stitches. Nothing major." The words scorched my tongue. My girl shouldn't *need* a couple of stitches. If anyone was jumping in front of flying weapons to save our charge, it should be one of us.

That thought had me shooting a hard glare at Steele, but he wasn't looking at me.

"I guess I'll go pack my stuff," Seph whispered, then hurried into the house with her arms wrapped around herself.

Steele stalked through the front door after her, not looking back at me, but there was a tension in his shoulders that made me hurry to catch up to him.

"Hey," I snapped, grabbing his arm as we entered the kitchen. Archer had placed MK down at the dining table and was pulling a medical kit out from the pantry. "What fucking gives, bro?"

Steele shot me a furious—*guilty*—glare, then continued over to MK. She tilted her head back as he paused in front of her, a soft smile on her lips.

"Don't do that," she said softly. "This wasn't your fault."

Anger seared through my veins. "I'm starting to think it fucking *was*. How the fuck did this happen, Steele? Why didn't you spot the threat?"

Steele stiffened, and Archer slammed the medical kit down on the table unnecessarily hard.

"Yeah, Steele," he snarled, "where the fuck were *you?*"

"Okay, that's *enough*," MK snapped. "I happened to spot the attacker first, so I shoved Seph out of the way, simple as that. Look, this isn't even bad." Reaching up, she gripped the knife and yanked it out, splattering Archer with her blood in the process.

"Fuck, babe!" I shouted, jerking into motion and tugging my belt free. In about ten seconds flat, we had secured it as a tourniquet just above the wound.

She gave me a sheepish smile and a small laugh. "Oops."

"This is my fault," Steele groaned, rubbing his hand over the back of his neck and grimacing. "I was distracted; I didn't even see the guy until Hellcat jumped on Seph."

Archer snapped. Before I could jump between them, his fist had slammed into Steele's face, and Steele went crashing to the ground.

"*Enough!*" MK shouted, sliding off the table and putting herself in front of Archer with a stubborn look on her face. "You hit him one more time and we're gonna have some *real* problems, D'Ath.

Take the medical shit, and go to the bedroom. *Now!*"

Her tone brokered no negotiation, cracking through the room like thunder, and Archer stiffened like *she'd* hit *him*.

"Archer D'Ath, if I have to repeat myself—"

"I'm going!" he snarled, then sent Steele a hard glare before stomping his angry ass away with the medical kit tucked under his arm.

When the bedroom door slammed behind him, MK shifted her gaze to me. "Do I need to put your ass in a time-out too, Kodiak Jones?"

I grinned and tried *really* hard not to *get* hard as she fixed me with that intense glare. Fuck me, she was sexy when she was all in charge and shit. So I just licked my lips and spread my hands in surrender as Steele slouched over to the freezer to grab ice for his face.

"Not unless that time-out includes spankings," I replied. My heart wasn't in the flirting, though, not while she was still drenched in her own blood and that tourniquet needed to be released sooner rather than later. "Go and let Arch patch you up, babe. He needs to care for you right now."

She eyed me suspiciously for another moment, then gave a short nod. Two steps saw her close the gap between us, then her soft hand cupped my cheek as she pulled me down to her level for a kiss.

"Don't bicker; it was no one's fault except the bastard

threatening Seph." She punctuated her order with another kiss that left my lips warm and tingling when she moved over to Steele.

He had a tea towel of ice against his cheek but lowered it when she rose up on her toes to kiss him too. His brow furrowed with a frown like he didn't think he deserved her kiss, but he quickly melted into her touch... just like we all did. MK was our kryptonite.

"We still have unfinished business," she told him in a sultry voice that told me *exactly* how Steele had been so distracted he'd missed a knife-throwing waiter approaching their table. Motherfucker. "Don't kill each other while I calm Arch down."

She gave me another hard look, but I just gave a small salute in response. I sure as shit couldn't promise her something like that, not when we were trying to remain honest with one another.

With a frustrated sigh, she grabbed a bottle of vodka from the freezer, then made her way down the hall to the bedroom where Archer was probably pacing a hole in the floor waiting for her.

Steele and I didn't move a muscle until we heard the door close softly behind her. Then I cocked a brow at him. "Distracted, huh?"

He blew out a long breath, guilt and regret all over his face. "I let my guard down."

"No fucking shit," I murmured. "We all did." Because Archer and I should have been there as well, not talking about our *feelings* outside the restaurant. But still... Steele knew better.

So I shrugged and decked him myself.

4

MADISON KATE

I could barely restrain my eye roll at the glare Archer gave me when I entered the bedroom. He was *such* a dramatic bitch sometimes, I swear, he gave Seph a run for her money.

"Don't look at me like that," I snapped, tossing the bottle of vodka over. He caught it effortlessly, and I went into the bathroom to grab a washcloth for my blood-streaked arm. Holy *shitballs,* it hurt.

He said nothing, but I'd barely even wet the washcloth before he was right there snatching it out of my hand and leading me back into the bedroom.

"Sit," he ordered, giving me a gentle push.

I scowled as my butt hit the mattress. "What'd I say about not being a fucking dog?"

His brow dipped in anger. "Then don't act like a bitch."

My jaw dropped. "You did *not* just say that."

Archer was pissed enough that he wasn't backing down, though. "What? You are. Clearly, we're just worried as fuck, and you're getting your claws out like—"

His rant cut off abruptly when I punched him straight in the nuts—his own damn fault for putting me right at groin height, and really it was barely more than a love tap since my dominant arm had a big old knife slice in it.

Still, he crumpled, clutching his crown jewels, and I hissed as my arm throbbed.

"Yep," he groaned, "I deserved that."

"Damn fucking right, you did," I growled. "Call me a bitch again, and I'll remove a testicle. Now, patch me up so I can stop whatever is going down out there." I nodded to the door and the fact that it seemed all too quiet. Had Kody already killed Steele?

Archer gave a pained laugh but shifted to his knees to open the medical kit beside me on the bed. "Yes, ma'am," he teased.

His touch was gentle as he cleaned up my arm and inspected the wound. It wasn't huge—the knife had stuck in, not sliced down—maybe only an inch or so wide, but deep. Ultimately, he decided it needed a couple of stitches, so he threaded up a needle while I gulped vodka.

"I could just give you painkillers, Princess," he commented as I cringed with the vodka burn.

I wrinkled my nose. "I'll take those too. But I'm guessing we need to haul ass to a new safe location soon, and I don't want to be completely out of it."

Archer shot me a lopsided smile as he held up the needle. "Oh, but drunk is okay?"

I shrugged. "I'm not drinking *that* much." But the first pierce of the needle through my skin made me groan and gulp down another huge mouthful of vodka in a desperate effort to numb the pain. Stupid fucking throwing knife. Luckily, I'd been training with the boys in the gym so much I actually had enough muscle in my bicep for the knife to stick into and not hit anything vital.

Archer murmured soft words of encouragement as he deftly stitched my wound closed, then swiped it with antiseptic and patched it up with a sticky gauze dressing.

"All done," he told me, packing away the supplies and gathering up a pile of bloody wipes to throw in the trash. "Unless you're hiding any other injuries I need to look at?"

The mood shifted in a breath, and a wicked smile curved my lips. The vodka in my belly might be partly to blame, but... okay, sure, I didn't need an excuse. We *were* married, after all.

"No injuries," I replied, "but I could use some help taking this dress off." I nodded to the mess of sticky, half-dried blood coating the side of my sundress. It was destined to go straight in the trash, unquestionably.

Archer gave me a knowing look and moved the box of medical supplies off the bed and out of the way. "I could probably help you with that," he commented. Rising to his feet, he offered me a hand up from the bed, then ever so carefully slid the straps of my dress over my injured shoulder.

The fabric clung to my side where the blood had started drying, but if anything, Archer only seemed *more* turned on rather than less as he peeled it free and dropped the dress to the floor.

"I think I can guess why Steele was distracted," he muttered, his hands cupping my breasts and his thumbs finding my hard nipples. "I fucking love that you don't wear a bra with those dresses, Princess. *So* fucking hot."

I gave a small moan, pushing my chest harder into his grip as my good arm looped around his neck. My fingers threaded into the back of his dark hair, and I tilted my chin up until our eyes met.

"Here's the thing," I whispered, leaning into his body, "the knife throwing waiter interrupted us before he could finish me off. So now, not only do I have fresh stitches in my arm, but I'm also dying a slow death of blue lady-balls."

His lips curled. "That sounds painful, Princess."

I groaned as he played with my nipples, my hand coming to the front of his shirt to unbutton it. "Excruciating," I replied, tugging his shirt off. "You wouldn't leave your wife in pain, would you?"

Archer stilled, his eyes flashing dark and dangerous. His hands left my breasts and smoothed down my sides to rest on my hips, his fingers hooked under the elastic of my panties.

"Say that again," he ordered, his voice thick with desire and underscored by dominance.

I wet my lips, knowing what had just flipped his switch. "Your *wife*, Archer D'Ath."

Yup, that did it. I gave a small, surprised scream as he ripped my panties clean off, then picked me up and dropped me into the middle of the bed. My arm throbbed, but it sure as shit wasn't bad enough to hold my attention when my *husband* was throwing his own clothes across the room like they were made of acid.

"Fuck," he muttered as he knelt between my legs, his fingers plunging straight into my depths. "You're drenched, Kate."

I moaned, spreading my legs wider as he pumped a second finger into me. "I told you. I was *right* about to come when that fucker attacked."

His lush lips curved as he stared down at me with raw hunger. "How badly does your arm hurt?"

"Um, what arm?" I asked, bucking my hips against his hand.

Chuckling softly, he pulled his fingers free of my desperate cunt and sucked them, then gently placed my arms above my head where we'd left a pair of leather cuffs yesterday.

"This okay?" he asked. Not because he was a sensitive petal concerned about my comfort—we were way past that—but because of my injury. Any other day, he'd have probably flipped me over and cuffed my wrists to my ankles without so much as a whisper of warning.

My arm hurt, no doubt, but it was going to hurt no matter what we were doing. So I nodded eagerly and waited impatiently as he buckled the cuffs to my wrists.

Once I was securely going *nowhere*, he leaned down and kissed me until I forgot how to breathe. Then he slammed his hard cock inside me with one brutal thrust. I cried out against his kiss, but he didn't let up, pulling out and thrusting in again just as hard. My teeth latched onto his lower lip, sinking in hard enough that I tasted the copper of his blood, and it just drove him wilder.

His hands hitched under my thighs, pushing my knees up toward my chest and spreading me wide. I groaned, squirming under his weight, and he sat up onto his knees to peer down at where we were joined.

"Lift your hips," he ordered, licking his lips and chasing the faint smear of blood there.

I did as I was told, and he shoved a pillow under my ass to support that angle. Then he gripped my thighs and went to fucking *work*. My wrists tugged and jerked in the cuffs as Archer fucked me hard, his gaze darting between my face, my bouncing tits, and the wet slide of his dick in and out of my pussy.

"Arch..." I said his name on a moan drenched in need.

He gave a husky chuckle. "I've got you, Kate. Try and keep

it quiet." His wink said he didn't expect me to do anything of the sort. When his fingers found my clit, rubbing at me while he continued fucking me hard, I detonated with a scream.

Archer grinned and quickly muffled my cries with his other hand over my mouth, but it was *probably* too little too late. Fucking *whatever*, I'd taken a knife today; I deserved to get my rocks off. Again. But in all seriousness, the orgasm was taking my mind off how much my arm hurt.

"Dammit, Princess," he chuckled when he peeled his hand away, kissing me instead, "so much for keeping you all to myself for a minute."

I was beyond words, though, moaning and panting, my hips bucking as I begged for more. Our tongues entwined as he kissed me deeply, his hands moving back to my breasts to toy with my nipples as his thrusts slowed to a less frenzied pace.

"Kate," he whispered in a hoarse voice as his kisses moved down my throat. His beard tickled my skin, making shivers of arousal zap across my flesh, and he found a nipple with his lips.

"Mmm?" I replied, my chest heaving as I fought to regain my breath.

He looked up at me, his ice-blue eyes holding my gaze as he licked a teasing circle around my nipple. "I love you, Princess."

A stupidly lovesick feeling swamped my chest, and my smile spread wide. "I love you, too, Sunshine."

"And I love both of you," Steele muttered, entering the

bedroom and closing the door behind him. He was already tugging his clothes off as he crossed the room to us. "But goddamn, you're loud when you come, Hellcat."

He kicked his pants aside and gave my cuffed wrists a hard look, then glared at Archer, who was still balls deep inside my pussy. "Really? She just got stabbed in that arm."

Archer gave an unapologetic shrug and sucked my nipple before replying. "She loves it, don't you, wifey?"

I just grinned. They both knew the answer to that.

Steele just rolled his eyes and unbuckled my wrists with easy, practiced motions as he sat against the headboard. "Come here, Hellcat," he purred, patting his lap, "we have unfinished business, remember?"

"Hey, what the shit, bro?" Archer protested but didn't stop me when I laughed and wiggled out from under him to straddle Steele instead. "Pretty sure my business was unfinished too."

Scoffing a laugh, Steele lifted me with his hands on my waist and impaled me on his long, pierced cock. I cried out again, way too freaking loud, and Archer reached out to gag me with his hand again.

Moaning, I leaned back against Archer's chest as I rode Steele's dick, in total bliss being sandwiched between their hot, hard bodies.

Archer kept his hand over my mouth for another moment, then whispered a curse and reached for the lube on the bedside table. "Sorry, Princess, this is gonna be a quick one."

He wasn't fucking kidding, either; within *seconds* he had me all lubed up and ready to go. This time Steele muffled my noises with his hand over my mouth as Archer pushed his thick cock into my ass.

"Is now a good time to tell you that Kody and Demi are in a pretty heated argument out there?" Steele asked with a smirk, addressing Archer over my shoulder.

Archer made a frustrated growl, giving a couple of shallow thrusts to warm me up a bit more. I was physically shaking with the overwhelming need to come again, though; I needed no warm-ups.

"So you thought this would be a great time to come blow your load?" he snarled, pumping into me a bit harder as his hands gripped my hips. "Don't get me started on—"

"Stop it," I snapped, yanking Steele's hand away from my mouth. "I don't want to hear another word out of either of you unless it's *I'm gonna come*. We clear?" I was panting, breathless, and couldn't stay still between them. I was so damn full of cock, but it was taking all my effort not to yell for Kody to join us.

They both muttered their acceptance, then I turned my head to lock lips with Archer as he found a rhythm in my ass while Steele fucked me from below. It was utter heaven. I swapped back and forth, kissing each of them as they tandem fucked me, making me come again *twice* before Archer unloaded inside me.

He muttered curses, but cleaned up and dressed. Steele and I continued, the two of us kissing and panting as I rode his pierced dick, chasing down my fourth climax. I looked back on my days where I'd struggled to come even *once* during sex and laughed. I'd just needed the right partners. Plural.

"I'll go sort things out with Demi," Archer told us. "But I won't stop Kody from crashing your party if you don't finish soon."

Sounded like a good time, if anyone asked me.

"Understood," Steele replied, then flipped us over so my back hit the mattress, and he sank back into my pussy from a position of dominance. "Holy shit, you feel good, Hellcat. I'm so fucking sorry I got you hurt today."

I moaned, arching into his touch. "Apologize in orgasms, Max. Make me come again, and all is forgiven." Because there was nothing to forgive.

"Done," he replied with a wolfish grin.

5

ARCHER

As much as it pained me to leave the room while Kate was still writhing all over Steele's cock, I had a burning need to speak with Demi myself about this whole fucking situation we were in. She was Seph's aunt, it made perfect sense for her to want to protect her niece. But she needed to do it without us. I wasn't risking my girl's life again, no way in *hell*.

"Where's Stacey?" I asked, frowning when I saw only Demi and Kody in the kitchen.

She shot me an irritated look, seeing as I'd just interrupted whatever she was saying to Kody. "Still cleaning up that mess in town," she snapped. "Because as *crazy* as it seems, that kind of shit isn't all that common around here. It's not as easy as it is in Shadow Grove to just make people look the other way when a man is dead in a restaurant."

Her tone was caustic and the resemblance to Hades was shockingly clear. It should have been enough to make me reconsider, but... fuck it. My girl was more important than the wrath of Hades.

"We're out," I announced. "I'm happy to get you and Seph set up at a new safe house, somewhere totally remote and off the grid, but then we're done. I'm not having Kate caught in the crossfire of Hades's war again."

Demi's brows shot right up, and Kody grimaced. He didn't contradict me, though. The tension in his folded arms and the hardness in his face said he was in agreement, no matter how bad of a business decision it was.

"Archer, that's a *very* stupid move, and you damn well know it. Hades expects you to keep Seph safe until—"

"Kate could have *died* today!" I roared, slamming my fist down on the table. "She could have fucking died, Demi, and for *what*? To protect a bratty teenager who doesn't even want to be protected? Let me spell it out for you. We're *done*. I won't risk Kate's safety for fucking *anyone*. Clear?"

"And what about Seph?" she shouted back at me, not backing down even slightly. "What about that innocent child who has *no idea* what kind of world she's really living in. What do you think would happen to her if Chase got his hands on her, huh? The shit that man would do just to control Hades—"

"It's not our fucking problem!" I bellowed. "It's not our job to keep her safe, and it's sure as shit not our problem that she's as clueless as a fucking rock."

"Archer D'Ath—" Demi snarled, her face hardening with fury, but Kody cut her short.

"That's enough," he said firmly. "From *both* of you. We're all tightly strung right now. Let's just take a fucking breath and work on a new safe location. Okay?"

My hands planted on the table, I sent him a dark glare, but he just met my gaze unflinchingly. Ballsy bastard was never scared of me, even when I was in a rage. Probably because he knew I'd never hurt him... not seriously.

Demi scowled. "I'm going to call Stacey. I don't like that she's at the police station alone." She stormed out of the kitchen, shooting me another scathing glare on her way.

"Well. That went well," Kody commented when we were alone. "Where the fuck is Steele?"

I snorted. "Where do you think?"

"Fuck," he snarled. "Like he deserves that right now."

"Shut the fuck up, bro," Steele replied, swaggering into the kitchen with a decidedly well-fucked look about him. "MK's asleep, so maybe quit the shouting for a bit?"

I scoffed and rolled my eyes. But, fair enough. Even if Steele hadn't just turned our quickie into a threesome, she'd have been exhausted. Probably best that she was sleeping and not witnessing me and Demi on the verge of throwing plates at each other.

"You both fucking suck," Kody sulked, stalking out of the kitchen.

"Don't wake her up!" Steele shouted after him, but Kody's only response was to flip him off.

Steele turned his scowl on me. "Did I hear that argument right? You want to quit the protection job?"

I shook my head, glaring back at him. "Don't fucking give me that face, bro. You want to tell me you're okay with this?"

He gave me an exasperated look, throwing his hands in the air. "No, of course not. But I'm also not okay with leaving a naïve teenage girl to fend for herself when some dickhead wants to hurt her simply to hurt her sister. It's not cool. And I guarantee MK won't stand for it either. Seph's her friend; she won't turn her back on her, *especially* now."

A long sigh escaped my lungs, and I sank down into one of the dining room chairs. "I know."

Steele's brows hitched. "Then what the fuck was that whole argument with Demi?"

"Wishful thinking?" I huffed in irritation. "I needed to blow off steam."

"And fucking our wife until she passed out wasn't good enough?" A teasing smile played over his lips, and I scowled harder to fight my own smile.

"She was awake when I left the room," I muttered back, swiping a hand over my short beard. "And she's *my* wife."

Steele scoffed with laughter. "Semantics, bro."

He poured us both mugs of crappy coffee—nothing like the liquid gold Kate made for us—and we sat down at the table to discuss our next move. Where to go. Who could be trusted not to leak our location like the owner of *this* safe house clearly had. Okay, maybe not the house itself or we'd be in shit right now, but certainly the vague location.

Eventually, we agreed on a plan. Kody hadn't returned, so we had to assume he'd either decided to nap with Kate or she'd woken up for the trifecta. Again. Damn girl was insatiable in the best way.

"Alright," Steele announced on a sigh, running his hand over his buzzed hair, "I might go and check on Seph to make sure she didn't hear you calling her a liability earlier. You and Demi were yelling pretty loud, and she shouldn't be made to feel responsible for MK getting hurt. Not when you and I both know *our wife* would do it again in a heartbeat."

I groaned. "Way to make me feel like an asshole." But he was right. Regardless of my own feelings about our assignment, whether we stuck with it wasn't my choice. Hell, nothing had been my choice since the moment Madison Kate had stepped back into my life... She owned me, mind, body and soul. There's nothing I wouldn't do to make her smile, even though I often had to make it difficult along the way.

Steele just gave me a pointed look, and I rolled my eyes skyward.

"Fine," I muttered, "I'll go check on the brat. I guess I should have kept my voice down a bit."

He grinned. "You think? I'll get on the phone with our friend in Poland to sort out a safer safe house."

I just nodded my response, agreeing that was the best option for safety and anonymity. No more tourist towns; we needed to go totally remote. With a sigh, I pushed up from the table and stomped my grumpy ass upstairs to Seph's room. Steele was right that I probably should have kept my voice lower, but it didn't mean I was wrong about anything I'd said.

Seph *didn't* want our protection. She thought her sister was massively overreacting because she was totally ignorant of the real danger. It sure as fuck wasn't my place to correct her either. But goddamn, it was growing infuriating to see her so careless.

I tapped my knuckles on her door, not wanting to bust in there and catch my wife's friend naked.

"Seph?" I called out. "It's Archer."

I waited for her response but heard nothing.

Frowning, I knocked louder. She might have headphones on.

"Seph, it's Archer. Can I come in?"

Silence.

A sinking feeling of dread filled me, and I shoved the door

open. Her room was empty; it barely took a quick glance around to confirm that. Just in case my gut was wrong, I checked the bathroom.

Nope. Just as empty.

What was worse? Her window was open and there was a note sitting on the bed.

"Fuck!" I roared, snatching up the note. "What the *fuck*?"

I clenched the paper in my hand and raced back downstairs to deliver the bad news. Seph had run away, and Kate was going to *murder* me.

Kate wasn't merely pissed. She stopped talking to me altogether. I could handle a lot of things from my girl. Dead silence and that stony stare that looked right through me was not one of them. It just pissed me off more.

We'd tracked Seph a couple of blocks from the villa before her trail went cold. Someone had to have picked her up. But who? She knew no one in Italy, as far as we were aware. The fact that she had no idea about what kind of real danger was out there didn't help matters. But Hades didn't want to hear about our fuckups. She wanted her sister found.

So Kody and I focused on the knife-throwing waiter—who he was and where he'd come from. We tracked down the waiter's gang or whatever the hell they called it here in Italy, I was sure they had some pretty fucking word for it. Then we'd torn through it and taken out most of the low-level punks, a few mid-levels, and moved on to interrogate the guy in charge.

"Maybe you should suggest that Hades give her sister some clue of what is going on. So she doesn't run off again. You know… if she's found," Kody offered.

He didn't know shit. They'd had a contract. It was apparently an open one. A lot of people were looking for the kid we were supposed to be protecting.

Fuck.

Me.

"Why don't you?" I asked him rhetorically. Hades didn't want our advice, and she sure as shit didn't want any of us poking around in her business. Her sister. Her decision. Just like informing Kate was my decision when I was the one withholding information.

"This is MK all over again," Kody grumbled. "She walked around blind because you wouldn't fucking tell her, and that *cost* us."

I just shot him a look. Did he think I didn't know that? I'd never forget her bolting from us and not only getting in a wreck but then getting stabbed. I didn't say anything, and he didn't push it.

We all knew.

They'd been up my ass to tell her about our secret marriage, and it'd taken my power-hungry older brother dropping it on her for her to find out some of the ugly truths. I shook my head. Zane was dead. Kate was safe. More than that, she was my fucking wife and she'd stay that way.

Whatever.

"No one knows anything," I muttered. "She's in the wind."

"She could be dead already," Kody mused, and I pivoted to stare at him. Seriously? "Right. Positive thinking. Let's find some more mafia types to beat up and kill. Nothing says we're serious like a trail of bodies."

That almost made me laugh, but no. We left the bloody mess of bodies behind us, and the building was going up in flames as we drove away. Demi was right; this wasn't Shadow Grove.

Our power only reached so far.

"Check on Kate," I ordered, and Kody snorted.

"Already done. Steele says she's still pissed and pacing the house. She went through Seph's room, though. Found some notes and what looks like a diary or maybe a travel journal?" Kody peered at his phone. "Or a sex book, since apparently she was documenting how often we got MK off."

That should not have made me laugh, but a rough chuckle escaped, even as Kody called Kate to check in with them. Two days. For two days we'd cut a swath across the village, the surrounding area, and two towns over. Demi had fucked off to who knew where without a word, and she'd taken Stacey with her. The only reason we hadn't abandoned the villa was on the off chance this proved to be Seph just running away and *not* being held somewhere.

It was that theory that kept Kate at the villa with Steele watching her. After she'd gotten hurt on his watch, he'd refused to leave her, and I couldn't blame him, even if I had in the immediate aftermath.

"What?" Kody asked, staring at his texts, and I cut a look at him. "Head back to the villa. They found Seph." Relief cut through me. "And she's a little bruised up but otherwise fine."

"Good, we can get Kate the fuck out of here."

6

MADISON KATE

Relief washed over me at Demi's words, and I sagged in my chair. Kody looped an arm over my shoulders, comforting me as I leaned into him. We were sitting around the kitchen table, my phone on speaker so everyone could hear.

"Thank fuck," I breathed. "How? Where was she? How did you get her out?"

Demi paused a moment before replying, and I got the feeling this was another case of *need-to-know* information. "She was being held in a warehouse in Sicily, but other than one bruise on her face, she seems relatively unharmed. Hades has arranged transport back to Shadow Grove for her, so you four are off the hook for babysitting duty."

Guilt rippled through me. We'd fucked up so bad. "Demi, I'm *so* sorry—"

"Don't worry about it," she cut me off. "I think we all know Seph does what Seph wants. Hopefully this scare is enough to set her straight, or things are going to get a lot worse."

Whatever *that* meant.

"Anyway, I should go," she continued. "Stacey and I are going to take a vacation, and I suggest you all do the same. I'm sure I don't need to point out that *none* of us are welcome back in Shadow Grove right now."

I winced and shot an accusing glare at Archer. After hearing about his blowup with Demi—that I'd somehow missed while Steele had fucked me into my fifth or sixth orgasm—I'd held him solely responsible for driving Seph off. If he hadn't run his big mouth, then she wouldn't have run off.

Okay, sure. I knew that wasn't true. Seph had run off because I'd been hurt and she didn't want to feel like a burden anymore. But I'd put money on it that Archer's argument with Demi hadn't helped matters.

"Thanks Demi," Steele replied, smoothing things over before the mood could deteriorate. "I think that's probably a great idea. We've been meaning to take a vacation, anyway."

Demi gave a long sigh on the phone. "Probably make it a long one. Hades... she's not happy. I wouldn't risk stepping foot back in

Shadow Grove without her permission right now. Just go check into a hotel somewhere and chill out until things blow over."

"Will do," Steele replied. "Keep Stacey safe."

Demi gave a low chuckle. "You know it."

She ended the call, and I continued glaring at Archer across the table.

"Don't fucking give me that look, Princess," he snapped. "This isn't my fault."

Kody snorted a laugh, and Steele wrinkled his nose in disagreement.

"It's not *not* your fault," Steele murmured. "But it's irrelevant. Seph's safe and on her way home to Hades. Job done. Let's discuss where we are going to lay low for a while."

Kody straightened up slightly, glancing to Steele at the end of the table. "Actually, I have a suggestion. If you guys are open to it, I was thinking maybe we could visit my mom. She's been driving me nuts wanting to meet MK, and I have some meetings with the Japanese KJ-Fit investors that I could take care of while we're there."

Excitement zapped through me, chasing away my anxiety in an instant. Kody's mom had lived in Japan for five years— since falling in love with it on a vacation—but developed a fear of flying so hadn't been back to Shadow Grove even once. Kody had mentioned his mom wanting to meet me plenty of times, and I'd spoken with her on video calls. But so far, we hadn't met in person. It was way past time that we made it happen.

"You wanna go to Japan, babe?" Kody asked, turning to me with a hopeful expression. "I think my mom is really going to like you."

I nodded eagerly but noticed the way Archer scowled at that statement. Maybe he disagreed?

"Alright, shit," Steele said with a yawn. "I'll sort out the flights. Probably best we get out of Italy now, anyway, considering the heat that will be coming down on us from the body trail we've left behind this week."

Archer just shrugged, unapologetic. "Had to be done."

I smiled, full of warm fuzzies that my guys had gone to such lengths to try and track Seph down. It didn't matter that we hadn't been the ones to find her. What mattered was that they'd given it everything.

Kody wove his fingers through mine and kissed my knuckles. "Just wait until you try the vending-machine canned coffee, babe. You're going to love it."

"Or hate it," Steele offered. "There's no middle ground."

Archer leaned in close and kissed my neck. "I'm going to fuck your ass on the flight over, just so we're clear."

Ugh, these boys. They spoke my love language unlike anyone else. Sex and coffee.

VAULT

Kody's mom lived in a small mountain village on Hokkaido, a two-hour train ride from Sapporo. In winter it was a ski village, but because we were there in summer, it was relatively quiet and devoid of tourists.

We'd been here a little over a week and had done a whole stack of sightseeing around Kody's business meetings. But today I just wanted to chill out and read a book in the sun for a bit. Clothed, of course, because I didn't want to get burnt and my arm was still tender, despite the stitches having been removed already.

The guys left me alone for the most part, too, and I found myself napping instead. Until my phone woke me up, anyway. When I saw the caller ID, I smiled and answered the call.

"Hey babe," I said warmly, "I feel like it's been forever since we spoke."

"Ugh, tell me about it," Bree replied. "I swear, every time I go to call you, Maddox kicks off a tantrum."

I grinned, lying back into the sun lounger I'd been napping on. "Where is my favorite godson now? I don't hear him in the background."

"Dallas took him out for a walk in the stroller," she told me with an exhausted sigh. "I swear to god, that man was made to be a father. He's like the baby whisperer."

"Aw, that's so cute." I laugh softly because in all the years I'd known Dallas, I could safely say I had never pictured him being dad-of-the-year material. Bree was right, though. He'd taken to

53

being a father like a duck to water. I'd never seen *either* of them so happy—albeit tired and rumpled.

Bree huffed. "You're damn right it is. You know what would be even cuter?"

I groaned because I knew exactly what she was going to suggest *again*. "I'm not reproducing just so that you have less cringeworthy parent friends to hang out with."

"Oh come *on*, MK. Just picture how cute a little baby Max Steele would be! Ugh, so adorable." She was off in fantasy land again, and it was far from the first time.

I snickered. "Oooh, I'm telling Kody and Arch you said their kids would be ugly."

Bree gave a dramatic gasp. "I did not! You're such a shit. Just fucking... ditch the IUD and see what happens. Your guys would make the cutest co-parents."

"You're fucking dreaming," I laughed.

"Come *on*," she wheedled, "cute little Wittenberg heir... You know you wanna see Arch go all alpha-daddy and shit."

I rolled my eyes. "You're right," I told her, teasing.

She gasped dramatically. "I knew it!"

Chuckling under my breath, I piled it on thick. "Uh-huh. Actually, now that you mention it, my breasts have been *crazy* sore lately, and I've been craving Japanese cheesecake something *wicked*. Bree, holy shit, I can't even remember when my last period was!"

"Boo, you whore," Bree muttered, catching onto my sarcasm finally. I had a hormonal IUD and hadn't had a period in years.

Just when I would have started laughing, movement in the corner of my eye caught my attention, and my gaze flew to Kody's wide eyes.

"You're *pregnant?*" he exclaimed, clearly in shock.

"Shit," I muttered, "Bree, I gotta go."

I stuffed my phone in my pocket and leapt to my feet, but Kody was quicker than me, racing back into the house and hollering for Arch and Steele. His mom was out, thank goodness, or this whole thing would end up a hundred times more awkward than it already was.

"Kody, shut up!" I yelled, hurrying after him. "Stop it; I'm not—"

"What's going on?" Archer demanded, bursting out of the living room, where he'd been doing push-ups or something. Steele was right behind him, his face twisted with worry as his eyes sought me out.

Kody spread his arms wide, giving me a hard look as though telling me to fess up. I rolled my eyes.

"Fuck me, you're *such* a dramatic bitch, Kodiak Jones. I'm *not* pregnant."

Steele's eyes went wide, and Archer stiffened like he'd just been shocked with a cattle prod.

"You *said*—" Kody started, stubborn defiance all over his

handsome fucking face.

"I was being sarcastic, you shortsighted fool," I shouted back. "Bree was being a shit about how we should have babies, and I was *teasing* her."

He folded his arms, clearly not believing me. Or not wanting to believe me. "You said your breasts were aching."

I scowled and yanked my shirt up to show them my tits—I wasn't wearing a bra *because* they were hurting. "Yeah, because *someone* was rough in bed yesterday."

Archer smirked, seeing his own teeth prints and fingermarks all over my breasts. "My bad," he muttered, sounding anything but apologetic.

Kody faltered, a frown creasing his brow. "Okay, but the cravings? We've all noticed how much Japanese cheesecake you've eaten this week. It's basically your main food group."

"Yeah, because it's fucking *delicious*. Jesus fuck, Kodiak, people are allowed to crave delicious foods without having a tiny human growing inside them." I planted my hands on my hips. Screw him, I hadn't eaten *that* much cheesecake.

Steele grinned. "She's got a point. I've probably eaten twice as much as her, and I'm pretty sure I'm not pregnant, bro."

Kody visibly deflated, his expression turning sad puppy. "But... the period thing? I thought when chicks miss their period—"

"Oh wow, even I know this one," Archer cut him off with a rueful smile. "Kate uses Mirena, bro. She doesn't get a period.

Remember she had it changed like eight months ago?"

I jerked in shock at that. "How do *you* remember that?"

He shrugged. "Because we had to use condoms for like a week or something."

I snorted a laugh. Of course *that* was why he remembered. The inconvenience of having to carry around condoms over that interim period while my new IUD settled in clearly stood out in his mind.

Kody gave me a sheepish look. "I did know that. Sorry. I guess I forgot. I heard what you said to Bree, and I just got... I dunno. Excited?"

I sighed, letting the defensiveness seep out of my posture. "Sit down, Kody. All of you, actually. Sit your sexy butts down and listen the fuck up." I planted my hands on my hips again and scowled until all three of them sat themselves on the couch. "Right. Now, I don't want to have this conversation every damn year for god knows how long, so I'm going to say this once and only once. Clear?"

All three of them nodded. I meant business, and they damn well knew it.

"Good." I paused for a moment, making sure I had their total attention. "I am not ready to be a mother. And *you three* are not ready to be fathers." They each looked offended by that statement in their own special ways, but I held a hand up to silence any impending protests. "Let me finish. I'm twenty-one years old. I am attempting to put myself through online business school so that one day I might be able to *run* my own *multibillion-dollar* corporate empire. But more importantly, I *like* our life. I *like* having sex whenever and wherever we want. I *like* not being tied to naptimes or feeding times or diaper changes or... fucking any of the other zillion things Bree has had to adjust to. I, for one, am not ready to give up what we have. Not any time soon."

I drew a breath to let that information sink in a bit deeper. This wasn't the first time we'd had vague debates about kids. But this time I was making sure I was firm and clear about my position, and they needed to respect that.

"You three hear the word pregnant, and it's like you time travel to the 1950s or something. This is the twenty-first century, for fuck's sake. A woman's *happily ever after* is no longer defined by her ability to snag a good husband and pop out babies. Those are personal choices for each individual woman, and should I ever decide I'm ready, they will *enhance* my fairy-tale ending, not define it. Are we clear?"

Silence was my only response.

Then, after a drawn-out moment, Archer cleared his throat. "So... you never want to have kids with us?"

Fucking idiot.

I threw my hands in the air. "That's *not what I just said, you moron!*"

Kody's brows shot up. "So you do?"

These three were going to be the death of me. I squeezed my eyes shut and rubbed the bridge of my nose while I tried to keep hold of my temper.

"Guys, chill," Steele intervened. "She's saying she's not ready *now*. Maybe someday, but no promises. Right, Hellcat?"

I nodded, gesturing in his direction. "Exactly. Just... ask me again when I'm thirty or something."

That seemed to placate them, and Archer pulled his phone out of his pocket. I frowned in confusion about who the fuck he would text in the middle of a conversation like this. But then my phone buzzed in my pocket.

I pulled it out, then groaned when I saw the notification on the screen. "You," I declared pointing my phone at Archer, "are impossible." Because who the fuck sends their wife a calendar invitation for her thirtieth birthday marked with *Baby Making Time?*

ARCHER

Kody had something really special planned for Kate, something he'd been thinking about for *years* now and something I knew he was equal parts excited and nervous about. And I couldn't even be a good, supportive friend to him about it because all I wanted to do was sulk like a little boy.

Fucking hell, I had issues.

She found me—I knew she would—when I was sitting out in Caroline Jones's pretty backyard feeding the overgrown goldfish in her pond.

"Hey, Sunshine," Kate called out, and I bit back a smile at the endearment. "Why are you sulking out here?"

I shot her a glare with zero heat behind it. "I'm not fucking sulking," I snapped. I was definitely sulking. But so what? I had a good reason.

She grinned and gave me a long look. "Sure you're not, you big baby. Stop feeding those damn fish; they look like they're going to sink soon."

I huffed but put my bag of fish food away. She was right... those fish were *fat*.

When I said nothing, she gave a frustrated sigh and grabbed my hand. "Come on, let's hash this out."

"Hash *what* out?" I grumbled, following along while she pulled me behind her. She was heading deeper into the garden, past the nicely manicured area and toward the forest. I hadn't explored this far around Caroline's property yet; both Kody and I had been busy with work shit almost every spare minute. But I knew Kate and Steele had been exploring together, so it was no real shock when a couple of minutes later she pushed me to sit on a bench seat in the middle of the fucking woods.

Random as hell, but whatever. I wasn't complaining when a moment later I had my wife straddling my lap, her hands clasping my face as she peered into my eyes.

"You're being a sour grump," she informed me. "Like, worse than usual. Ever since we arrived in Japan, too. You got a problem with sushi or something?"

I scowled. "Sushi is delicious."

She flicked a grin. "No shit. So what's your damn problem? Have I not been sucking your dick enough lately or something? 'Cause I gotta be honest, I'm starting to get lockjaw from all the blow jobs I've been giving out."

Goddamn, my dick for hardened at just the *mention* of blow jobs. What was I, fucking fifteen? Christ. Clearing my throat, I shifted her in my lap so my erection wasn't *so* obvious. "You think you're funny," I muttered, wetting my lower lip, "but you know full well there's no such thing as too much dick sucking."

Her grin turned sexy, and I groaned inwardly. I couldn't fucking resist her in this sort of mood. Hell, who was I joking? I couldn't resist her in *any* mood.

"So, what I'm hearing, Sunshine, is that if I get your dick out right now and wrap my lips around it... you'll tell me why you've been such a mopey bitch since we arrived here?" She arched a brow in question, but her fingers were already working my belt undone. My girl didn't mess around with empty promises when it came to sex, that was for fucking sure.

I gave in to the grin creeping over my lips but snatched her hands away from my crotch, instead pinning them behind her back.

"Princess..." I rumbled, catching her chin with my free hand. "I'm not a mopey bitch."

She rolled her eyes. Sassy didn't even begin to touch on my woman's attitude. "Okay sure, I totally believe you." The sarcasm was thick enough to choke on.

But still, my mopey ass was just having a jealous moment over something that wasn't my secret to reveal. As badly as I was feeling sorry for myself, I was also emotionally stable enough to recognize Kody's right to surprise our girl himself. I wasn't going to ruin that just because the green-eyed monster was rearing its ugly head.

Kate was *so* good at getting me to spill my guts, though. I needed to change the subject before I ruined everything.

"How are your assignments going?" I asked, grasping onto the first topic that *wasn't* Kody's surprise... or her lips around my dick. Blame it on the therapy we'd all been to after Kate's ordeal eighteen months ago, but I'd been actively working on our connection outside of the bedroom—which wasn't as easy as it sounded when the chemistry between us was so fucking electric. Even now, trying to ask her about her course work, I couldn't seem to release the hold on her wrists. She was mine.

Her lips curled, but she played along. "They're hard," she admitted, "but that's okay. I kinda like when things get hard."

Oh sweet Jesus. That wink.

My grip on her wrists tightened, and her breath caught as she gave me a hungry look. Dammit, my dick was so hard it was actually hurting against my jeans.

"Princess," I growled, "we're—"

"In the middle of the forest with no one around to see?" she finished sweetly, batting those long lashes. "Besides, every time I talk to you about my assignments, your eyes glaze over and I can tell you're bored as shit."

She wasn't wrong. Academic learning wasn't my strong suit, and when she talked to me about the intricacies of the MBA she'd been working toward by correspondence, it made me feel dumb as fuck. Not that I was actually stupid; my strengths just lay in different areas.

"I'll cut you a deal," she offered, suggestive as a fucking siren.

I couldn't resist. "I'm listening…" I still held her chin and used that grip to bring her face closer, brushing my lips ever so softly over hers.

Victory flashed through her eyes, and it hardened my cock even more. Shit if I knew how *that* was even possible; I was like granite already.

"Let me ride your dick right here out in the woods," she whispered, her voice dripping with desire and mischief as she rolled her hips against my crotch, "all vanilla and boring like we're a *normal* couple in love… and I'll insult you while you spar with Kody later."

A rough laugh bubbled out of my chest, and I grabbed her lips in a hard kiss. She knew what made me tick. "Counter offer," I replied, refusing to agree so easily, no matter how good her plan sounded. "In addition to heckling me through training, I want a public argument with name calling."

She grinned broadly. "Deal, I'll even throw my drink at you if you're lucky."

Well shit, how's a guy supposed to say no to an offer like that? Bickering and throwing insults was our love language, and the sex afterward was always phenomenal. Not that *any* sex with Kate was dull, but she really let her freak flag fly when we were coming off a raging argument. The shit she'd let me do to her after we'd ripped into one another in the middle of a restaurant... Goddamn.

She knew she had me; her lips met mine as a groan of anticipation reverberated between us. I kissed her back with all the hunger and desperation of the very first time we'd kissed. Every kiss between us was the same; I would never get sick of her soft lips on mine. The little gasps she made as I coaxed her mouth open went straight to my heart, and my dick, and I could die a happy man just for having that simple connection of a kiss with this girl.

"Archer," she moaned as my kisses moved to her throat, my teeth scraping over her delicate skin. Her hips rocked against me, her hot core grinding against my jeans even as I still held her wrists pinned behind her. Fucking hell, Madison Kate *D'Ath*—as she would forever be in my mind—wouldn't know the meaning of vanilla sex if it came up and bit her on the ass.

Giving in to what she wanted—what we both wanted—I released her wrists just long enough to reach under her skirt and relieve her of the flimsy tie-side panties she'd taken to wearing after getting grazes from us ripping lace panties off too often. These things she wore now were probably designed for strippers, but I sure as fuck wasn't arguing. Talk about easy access.

She moaned and gasped as I stroked my fingers over her bare pussy, and I felt my lips curling with a satisfied grin. I'd never get sick of this. Never.

Her hands made quick work of my belt and fly, and a second later, it was my turn to moan when her delicate fingers wrapped around my cock. She wasn't tentative about it; she knew what she wanted and how to best get it. And that sure as shit wasn't to treat me *gently*. No, she gripped my dick with determination, her fist pumping down my length firmly as I grunted and tried really damn hard not to blow my load all over her hand like a virgin.

To take my mind off my own intense arousal, I flicked my thumb over her clit and watched her squirm. *Fuck yeah, that's it.*

I did it again, then pushed two fingers deep inside without any warning. She gave a startled cry, but the shudder that rolled through her body and the way her hips pushed down onto my hand told me I was on the money.

"Fuck," she hissed, riding my hand as I pumped my fingers. She was so damn wet it was driving me wild. "Dammit, Arch, I want your dick."

Sweetest damn words I'd ever heard.

Withdrawing my fingers, I let her rise up on her knees just enough to notch my tip at her entrance. Fuck me, the control it took not to just slam up into her when that scorching wet heat was right there on the crown of my dick... torture.

But I didn't because it was torturing her just as much as me. And I lived for those little whimpers and moans she made when she was desperate for my dick.

"Arch," she moaned, writhing in need as I tightened my grip on her hips, preventing her from sinking down onto my shaft.

I grinned. "Kate."

She gave a noise of sheer frustration and desperation, but the smile tugging her lips said she enjoyed the game just as much as I did. "Fine," she snarled, her eyes blazing as they met mine. "I love you, you infuriating sack of shit."

My heart soared.

"I love you, too, you bratty Princess," I told her in a husky whisper, releasing her waist so I could tangle my fingers in her silky blonde hair. "Now fuck me like you hate me."

She barked a laugh, then crashed her lips against mine as she slammed down onto my dick. Both of us gave long moans at that first strike, and her pussy hugged my dick so hard I thought I was never going to get it back. Then she started to rise and fall, riding me like a woman on a mission, and I just held on for dear life.

Our tongues danced, fighting for superiority, and the noises she made were pushing me way too fucking close to coming early. I needed to flip the tables, or this really would be a boring quickie. Emphasis on *quick*.

I let her fuck me a little while longer, distracting myself by pulling her hair and pinching her nipples through the thin fabric of her dress. When her movements came faster, shallower, I knew she was about to come. So I gritted my teeth and lifted her off my lap.

"What the fuck, Arch?" she snarled like a pissed off tigress. Goddamn, that was hot.

I just snickered and stood up. Her brows instantly lifted, and without any instructions, she leaned forward to brace her hands on the back of the bench seat.

"That's my girl," I praised, stroking my dick with one hand, loving how wet it was from her pussy. I flipped her short skirt up over her ass and grabbed onto her hip as I slammed my dick home inside her once more. We groaned in unison again, and I shifted my grip onto the perfect globes of her ass.

Kate rocked back onto my dick, making me hiss as I shifted my feet to kick hers wider.

"Is that all you've got?" she taunted, panting and breathless but full of sass when she turned her face to catch my eye. "Come on, Sunshine, fuck me like you hate me."

Ugh, fuck. There was that wink again. Little shit.

My hand cracked across the swell of her rear before I'd even finished forming the thought, and she howled. Her pussy contracted around my cock in the most incredible way, so the second her muscles released, I had to repeat the gesture. Again and again, until her behind was pink and glowing and her pussy was quite literally dripping she was so turned on.

Grinning at the whimpers and choked curses falling from her lips, I slowed my hips. I circled my dick with my fingers, swiping up the wetness of her arousal to slick over her backdoor. She shuddered and moaned, her back arching, but she stayed perfectly still as I pushed my index finger into that tight space.

My teeth gripped my lower lip so hard I could taste blood and I was so damn close to coming it was insane, but my girl had given me an order. She wanted it rough and dirty, and I was nothing if not a slave to her desires.

"Arch," she gasped, pushing back onto my dick and fingers as I added a second one. "Archer, fuck. Yes." Whatever else she was saying faded into a long moan as I pumped my fingers, stretching her ass wider. Goddamn, I wanted to claim it with my dick right here in the forest. But there was no way I could hold out that long, and I wasn't rash enough to fuck her ass as hard as I wanted to without lube. Only dickhead amateurs who didn't give a shit about their girl's enjoyment pulled a stunt like that.

"You gonna come for me, Princess?" I asked in a breathy growl, working my fingers in time with my cock. Fuck yeah. She was about to go off. Her knuckles were white against the back of the seat, and her knees were already shaking.

Her angry retort was lost between gasps and moans, but I got the gist of it. She'd lectured me enough that women don't just come because they're told to. She didn't *need* me to tell her... she was holding it off on her own. But even she had her limits.

My hips slammed harder and harder against her, my fingers pounding her back hole, and moments later she was howling her release.

Thank *fuck*.

I could have sworn my soul had left my body for a hot second when her pussy constricted around my cock. She fucking *owned* me, and I was helpless to do anything but climax right alongside her. I grunted deep and low as my dick jerked inside her steel grip, unloading right inside that sweet cunt.

The argument we'd had about kids earlier was still fresh on my mind, but shit if I couldn't argue with her reasoning. Nine more years of this level of sexual freedom? Hell yes, sign me right the fuck up.

She groaned as I slipped free of her body, arching a sly look at me from over her shoulder. "That was terrible," she teased. "Worst sex of my life."

I grinned, snatching her by the wrist, then kissed her until her knees gave way and she sagged in my grip.

Kate was my soulmate. My perfect match. Babies or not, she was my queen. My forever. Nothing could ever change that.

8

KODY

My eyes were glued to the forest behind my mom's garden where I'd seen MK and Archer disappear an hour or so ago. She'd said she wanted to find out why he was sulking, but I hadn't expected them to be gone quite this long.

"Settle down, Kody," my mom told me with a laugh as she stepped out onto the back porch with me. Her hand was wrapped around a mug of green tea, and her eyes were brighter than usual. In a good way, though. "Archer knows what you've got planned, he won't keep her out there too long."

I huffed and rolled my eyes. She had way more faith in Archer than I did. He was all kinds of jealous right now, and I wouldn't put it past him to sabotage my surprise.

Ugh, no, that wasn't true. He and Steele were closer than just my best friends; they were my brothers. Even when we were so jealous we couldn't see straight, we wouldn't actively ruin each other's special moments with our woman. It was why this thing between the four of us worked so well. We *all* loved each other, even if we were too macho to openly admit it.

"Look, here they come now," my mom pointed out, nodding toward the edge of the forest.

Sure enough, MK and Archer were emerging from the trees looking ruffled and well fucked. God damn him to hell. He might not have ruined my surprise, but he was sending her back to me coated in his touch. Asshole.

"Hey, babe," she called out with a bright smile as they came closer. Her lips were red and puffy, and there was a distinctive beard rash on her cheeks. Fucking Archer and his facial hair. "Were you waiting for us?"

Archer glowered, but when I glared back, he gave me a lopsided smile. "I'll catch you two later," he murmured. He pulled MK close, kissing her way longer than necessary before he stalked toward the house once more.

He mumbled a cool but polite greeting to my mom on the way past but disappeared quickly. Archer wasn't a huge fan of my mom... for good reason. But at least he just avoided her instead of starting fights like he used to do when we were teenagers.

MK stopped on the step below where I stood, peering up at me with curiosity all over her flushed face. "Are you okay? You seem... tense."

Shit. I needed to chill the hell out.

Offering her a smile, I held out my hand. "Yeah, totally. I just thought maybe we could take a walk together? I've been so busy this week; I really want to just spend some time alone with you."

Her smile brightened, and she took my hand. "Of course!" Then she wrinkled that adorable nose of hers. "Uh, could I maybe just wash up quickly?"

It was on the tip of my tongue to say no—we were already running late—but I also knew what her and Arch had been up to in the forest. So I gave her a tight nod, and she hurried past me with a promise she'd be quick.

"Take a breath, Kody," my mom suggested when MK was gone, giving me a quick, one-armed hug. "I'll keep going with the plans for tomorrow."

I exhaled heavily. "Thanks, Mom."

She smiled up at me, then headed back inside. It'd taken us a long time to get to this place, but we'd reconnected not long before I met MK and been working on our relationship in baby steps since then. That was all part of the story I wanted to tell my girl on our walk, anyway.

True to her word, MK came clattering back down the stairs five minutes later in a fresh change of clothes and still smelling of soap from the shower. She beamed at me and took the hand I offered, weaving our fingers together as we left the house.

"Okay, so I get the feeling this is more than a casual need to spend some alone time," she accused when I made no attempt to start a conversation. She knew me so well.

Flashing her a quick smile, I tugged her closer so I could kiss the side of her head. "You'd be right." I drew a breath, leading her away from the village and onto a walking track. "I know I've been super busy this week, but I wanted to... I dunno. Explain the weirdness with my mom, I guess."

She gave me a soft smile. "You really don't need to, you know? I sort of figured if you'd wanted to rehash the messy details, you'd have told me by now."

I winced. She was totally right; I *should* have told her by now. We'd been together for two and a half years. It was *past* time.

"My mom is a recovering addict," I blurted out before I could lose my nerve.

She arched a brow. "I know."

Of course she did; I'd told her *that* part ages ago when I'd explained about my mom living in Japan. I'd already told her all about how my mother had made a choice to get clean and sober, met a man in rehab who'd been a travel journalist, then how she'd fallen in love with Japan and decided to stay. Without the guy.

But I never had told her the reason my mom got sober. Or how I'd ended up living with Archer and his dad when I was twelve. I didn't really have any good reason *not* to have told her, but having her meet my mom in person had it on my mind.

"Right," I murmured. "Yeah. You know how I told you my dad died when I was two?"

She nodded. "Heart attack, right?"

"Yep. So Mom started out with antidepressants, then antianxiety pills, then when they weren't erasing her pain enough, it all just escalated from there. Shit was pretty rough for a while, but my grandma used to visit once a month and restock the pantry... things like that. She tried to take me back to Texas with her a thousand times, but my mom would just totally freak out and scream about how she'd already lost enough." I paused to collect my thoughts. I never, ever talked about my childhood, so it was hitting me a bit too hard in the feels.

MK just leaned into me, her arm linked around my waist as she offered silent support. Fuck, I loved her.

"When I was eleven or so, a dealer came to the house looking for my mom. She owed him a whole stack of money, but when he couldn't find her—she wasn't home—he took me as payment." I'd never really told anyone this story before. It hurt. Fuck me, it still hurt.

MK tugged on my hand, leading me over to a fallen tree trunk, and pushed me to sit down. When I did as she wanted, she climbed right on into my lap and wound her arms around my neck.

"Kody," she whispered, her voice full of pain and anger, "I

could ki—"

"Let me finish," I murmured gently. "Otherwise, I'll never get the whole story out. And I want you to know all my damage before..." My mouth went dry. I was such a little bitch sometimes.

She frowned, worried for me, but nodded silently. Her body remained curled around me, though, and I held her tight as I wet my lips to continue. Having her in my arms grounded me, reminded me that this crap was ancient history.

"This shady fuck grabbed me, a skinny little malnourished kid, and tossed me in the back of his truck. Took me back to his place and locked me up in a kennel. For a whole week he treated me like just another of his dogs, feeding me tinned dog food and making me drink from a bowl." I winced, my stomach clenching and flipping at the memory.

MK's fingers stroked the back of my neck, soothing me. "Then someone rescued you?" she asked softly. Hopeful.

I shook my head. "No. Then he dragged me out in the middle of some kind of party at the back of his property and tossed me into a caged area. He told me if I won the fight, I could go free." I paused to draw a breath and to separate myself from the emotions tied to that dark memory. "He lied. I was desperate, terrified, starving... but I won. Then he just laughed and said I was too valuable to set free now."

"How long?" she asked, her brow creased deeply with concern.

I reached up to smooth that line away with my thumb. "I don't know. But then one night Archer and his dad were there. After the fight, Arch broke me out and demanded Damien take me home with them. For all Damien's faults, he wasn't a total bastard. He saved me that night... even if it was just because he saw a potential new Reaper."

MK was silent for a long time, her forehead resting on my shoulder and her body wound tightly around mine. I was okay with that too. Nothing comforted me more than having her in my arms. Besides, this was ancient history. And it had introduced me to Arch and Steele, so I couldn't complain.

After a while, she raised her head and met my eyes with determination shining in hers. "Kodiak Jones," she murmured, "you're amazing. That... what you went through, being treated like that and having to fight countless men just to—"

I cringed and shook my head. "No. Not men."

She quirked a brow in question, and I exhaled heavily.

"He didn't make me fight people... he threw me into *dog* fights."

Shock rippled over her face, and her hand shifted down to my forearm where I had dozens of small, faded scars hidden by tattoos. Yeah. Dog bites.

"That sick fuck," she breathed. Then her expression shifted to murderous. "Your mom—"

"She was unwell," I quickly cut her off. "It took me a *really* long time to understand this. But she was in an awful place inside her own mind. She needed professional help, and there was no one around who cared enough to get it for her. Even when my grandma visited, she didn't pay enough attention to see what was really going on. My mom didn't put me in the dog fights—hell, she didn't even knew who'd taken me, she thought I'd run away. She was just... neglectful. And she's had to come to terms with that on her own over the last decade or so."

MK said nothing, her teeth worrying at her lower lip as she frowned. I could feel how tightly wound up she was, like she wanted to run back to the house and punch my mom in the face. It was why I'd wanted to go for a walk while we talked. Or... part of the reason.

"You guys seem so okay now," she said eventually. "I never would have known... except maybe for the way Arch and Steele are around her."

I gave a lopsided smile. "Yeah, they're... Well, you know how they are. But they were also really supportive when my mom reached out a few years ago. It took me ages to decide I wanted to get to know her again, but when I made my mind up, they stood by my decision."

She gave me a long look, searching my eyes like she could see right through to my fucking soul. I had nothing to hide from her, though, so I let her see it all—the pain that those memories brought me, but also the calm confidence in my own growth since that time. From the moment Damien D'Ath had taken me under his wing, had blooded me into his gang, I was a different person.

That weak, feral boy had long since gone.

Her hands came up to cup my face, then her sinfully soft lips were against mine. I sighed into her kiss, pulling her closer and kissing her deeper. I loved how physical she was. Her verbal communication skills sucked almost as bad as Archer's, but she conveyed so much with her body and her touches.

"I love you, Kody," she whispered against my lips some minutes later. We were both breathing heavily, and I was hard as a damn rock beneath her. Like it could be helped when she was grinding all over me and making those sexy little moans while we kissed.

I smiled, my heart light as a feather. "I love you more, babe," I replied, kissing her again. I stopped before we could start stripping down to fuck on the side of the path, though. Despite how innocent my choice of a walking trail seemed, I *did* have a surprise waiting for her. The sun had fallen below the horizon now, but the night was clear enough we would have no problems finding our way.

"Come on," I urged, lifting her to her feet and linking our fingers. "There's a waterfall at the end of this track that I want to show you."

She leaned into me as we walked, and I had to acknowledge how freeing it'd felt to tell her that last dark corner of my past. It was history and had no bearing on the future, but there was something so incredibly uplifting about knowing we truly held no more secrets. MK was my girl. She was *it* for me... It felt right for her to know everything about me.

Besides, I needed her to know about my mom.

As we reached the end of the path, the sound of rushing water filled the air around us. A moment later, we stepped out onto a curved wooden bridge over the pool at the base of the waterfall, and thousands of fairy lights flickered to life in the trees surrounding us.

MK gasped, looking around with eyes full of awe. "Kody," she breathed, her smile bright as she took in the picturesque setting. "This is gorgeous. Did you plan this?"

I just smiled, because *yeah*. My mom had helped, too. In response, I fished the ring out of my pocket and sank to one knee.

The shock that rippled over her face made me chuckle, and she pressed her fingers to her lips.

"Kody, what the... Are you..." Her voice was high and tight, and I could see her pulse hammering in her throat.

I grinned wider, taking her hand in mine to thread the ring onto her finger. It fit snug against the D'Ath heirloom ring that Archer had given her almost two years earlier. I'd had it custom made to match.

"Madison Kate Wittenberg," I said softly, nervous excitement running through my whole fucking body. My damn hands were shaking where I held hers, I was so tense. "Will you marry me?"

She blinked at me, silent. It was something we'd discussed not long after her stalker had been killed, how we would get forged documents to allow us all to marry her one day. But it hadn't been mentioned since then, so maybe she thought we'd changed our minds? Shit, I definitely hadn't. Neither had Steele... no matter how pissy Archer was about *officially* sharing her.

When she just stared, frozen, I started to second guess myself.

Fuck. Had I totally misread things...?

"Uh, babe, this is the part where you reply," I prompted with a slightly awkward laugh.

She blinked rapidly, like she was snapping herself out of something. Then shook her head.

"Kody," she groaned, sounding... apologetic? Shit. *Shit.* "I can't..."

9

MADISON KATE

Holy motherfucking shitballs. Kody's proposing! He has a ring!

"Kody..." I groaned in awe, totally in shock. "I can't believe you went to all this trouble for me!" Grabbing his wrist, I pulled him to his feet, then launched myself into his arms. "Yes, of course I'll marry you! How was that ever even a question?"

The exhale of relief that gusted out of Kody confused the hell out of me. Had he really thought I was going to say no? Fuck that, I would marry him right here and now if he wanted.

The desperate way he kissed me, though, told me he'd been worried. Silly penguin should know better than that. As far as I was concerned, we were already together till we died.

Then a thought crossed my mind, and I gasped as I pulled away.

"Is this why Archer is in such a mood today?"

Kody grinned. "Yeah. He's a jealous little bitch who liked being the only one you were legally married to."

I groaned and rolled my eyes. "Typical fucking Sunshine." I bit my lower lip and looked around us once more. Lights twinkled in the trees all around the waterfall and reflected gorgeously off the water of the pool below our bridge. "You did this all for me?"

Kody looped his arms around my waist as I turned to take it all in, hugging me from behind as I leaned on the bridge railing. "Of course. I thought... maybe, if it's okay with you, we could have the ceremony while we're here in Japan."

Surprise rippled through me, and I turned around to face him. "This week?"

His brow creased with uncertainty. "Too soon?"

I grinned. "Not soon enough!"

His answering smile lit up his whole face, then he was kissing me until I forgot where my lips ended and his began. Fuck it, who cared? I'd happily never separate from him for the rest of my life. Getting married would just be a formality, but it was clearly important to him. So it was important to *me*.

Carolyn spent the next few days hard at work behind the scenes arranging everything for our wedding. That Saturday, I married my penguin in a small Shinto ceremony with just Kody's mom and my bio-dad James as witnesses. Oh, Arch and Steele were there too, of course. But that was it, and that was all I needed.

Neither of us were *actually* Japanese, so we didn't want to borrow too heavily on their customs, but I did wear a stunning red gown with gold embroidery detailed around the hem and collar. It was perfect. Everything about it was *perfect*. Even the fact that Kody not-so-subtly high-fived Steele while we kissed at the end of the ceremony.

I had been somewhat awkward around Carolyn since hearing the story of Kody's childhood, but by the time our wedding day celebration wrapped up, I had to admit… she was trying. She clearly regretted her past and was doing her best to make amends with her son now.

Ultimately, Kody wanted a positive relationship with her. So I would follow his lead and focus on the present, not the past.

That night, when we all stumbled home sake-drunk *hours* after Carolyn and James had gone home, Kody could barely wait until we got inside to pin me to a wall.

"Fucking hell," Steele groaned as I moaned into Kody's kisses. "You're killing us, Hellcat."

"Me?" I protested between kisses, my hands already at Kody's pants and stroking his hard dick through the fabric. "Why?"

Archer's response was to grab my hair and tug my lips free of Kody's and onto his instead. His mouth claimed mine hard and fast, then he released me with a groan. "I love you, Princess." He kissed me again, softer this time, then abruptly stalked away further into the house.

A moment later, a door slammed, and loud music started playing.

"I'm... confused," I admitted.

Kody chuckled, kissing my neck. Steele ran a hand over his buzzed hair and shrugged.

"You'd think after this long he'd be less of a little bitch about sharing," Steele commented with a laugh. Then he stepped in close and pressed a tender kiss to my lips. "But he had a good point. I love you as well, Hellcat."

"And I love you," I murmured back, still crazy confused. "All of you."

Steele clapped Kody on the shoulder, then headed off in the direction Archer had gone.

"Kody, what—" I started to ask, but he cut me off with more drugging kisses. He swept me up into his arms, and I let out a small squeak of surprise as he started carrying me up the stairs.

He strode down the hall and nudged open the bedroom door to reveal the most romantic scene I could have imagined—even more so than the fairy-lit waterfall he'd proposed in front of. The whole room was lit with dozens of candles—such a fire hazard—and beside the bed there was a bottle of champagne in an ice bucket. Not that we needed more wine after all the sake.

"Kodiak Jones... are you kidding? When did you become such a romantic?" I exclaimed as he gently set me down on my feet.

He gave a small laugh, turning me around to unzip my dress. "Um, probably since I fell in love."

Oh man, my heart.

He dragged my zipper all the way down, and the fabric slipped from my body with ease, leaving me in just my bright red bra and panties. Kody gave a low groan and kissed the bend of my neck as he unhooked my bra and tossed it aside.

"Get on the bed," he told me in a husky voice. "Against the pillows."

I bit my lip with excitement and did as I was told, crawling up the bed in what I hoped was a sexy kind of way, then settled into the middle to watch him undress himself. He took his time with it, too, giving me a show with each button that slipped free.

By the time he was naked, I was panting and flushed with heat.

"Kody," I moaned, rubbing my thighs together. "I need you."

Grinning, he came around to the side of the bed. His dick was hard and glistening with pre-cum, but he was in no hurry. Without a word, he took some black silk scarves from the drawer and bound my wrists to the headboard while I desperately tried to control my own anticipation.

When he was satisfied with the binding, he tied a soft black blindfold over my eyes.

"Comfortable?" he asked with a teasing tone as the bed dipped under his weight.

I smiled in his general direction. "I'd be more comfortable with your dick inside me, but I guess this is okay for now."

He laughed in response, then made me gasp as his lips closed over one of my nipples. "I wanted to play a little," he confessed, "seeing as it's our wedding night. Also, because Arch and Steele promised to leave us alone for the whole night so I don't have to share you with anyone."

Ah, that explained the weirdness downstairs.

"I thought you liked sharing me," I replied, my pussy hot with arousal just thinking about it. I'd admit, I was fairly fond of the sharing myself.

Kody took his time, sucking my hard nipple into his mouth while his fingers tugged on the other, making me writhe under his touch.

"I do," he eventually replied. "But I also love having you all to myself. Wife."

I smiled wide at that. I loved that he'd wanted to make things *official*… as official as they could be, anyway. "So, what are you going to do with me now, husband?"

His response was to pull away slightly, a cool breeze replacing his body warmth for a moment. Then he was back, and this time when his lips closed over my nipple it was a whole different sensation.

I gasped sharply at the temperature change and moaned

when he rolled the ice in his mouth over my tight peak. Oh. Now the blindfold made sense… He wanted to play with ice.

Then heat flashed through my other breast, and I cried out in surprise.

"You okay, babe?" Kody murmured, kissing the curve of my breast as the sudden heat faded down to a dull warmth.

I nodded quickly, feeling the tightness of hardening wax on my skin, and found my voice. "Y-yes. Fuck. I didn't expect that."

He chuckled. "That's kinda the point, babe."

I groaned. He really did want to play. "Kody… I need you inside me." Like *now*, not later.

"Patience is a virtue, gorgeous," he replied, teasing, then drizzled a hot line of wax between my breasts. This time I was prepared and didn't cry out. My breath definitely caught, though, and my cunt flushed so hot I could feel my panties soaking through.

Thankfully Kody tugged the red thong away a moment later, leaving me bare and spread open for whatever he had planned. For a minute, he didn't touch me. Didn't speak or move. I knew he was still there because I could hear his breathing, but he was just driving me wild with anticipation.

"Kodiak Jones," I growled as my frustration snapped. "If you don't touch me, I swear to fuck—"

I cut off my threats as hot wax dripped across my pubic bone and made me almost swallow my tongue. Then it was ice on my clit, and I damn near exploded.

"Like this?" Kody asked, his voice rough and heavy. "Touch you like this, babe?"

I was incapable of words. I just moaned and nodded, bucking my hips up into his touch as he slid the melting ice lower.

"How about this?" he breathed, sliding the ice inside my pussy. I was so hot down there it would melt in no time, but he must have thought the same thing because he immediately added a second cube and pushed it deep with two fingers.

Gasping, I rocked my hips to urge his fingers to move, but he had a different idea. A better idea. He fingers slipped out, but a moment later his huge cock filled me, pushing the ice deeper and making me scream.

"Oh shit," he groaned, shifting his weight onto his elbow beside my head. His hand hitched under my thigh to lift my leg higher, giving him a deeper angle. "Fuck yes, let's melt that ice, babe."

Holy hell, like I needed telling twice. I was already spiraling into mega-orgasm territory, my pussy clenching him tight and my heart racing. When he started moving, thrusting into my cool pussy, it wasn't slow or teasing. Nope, Kody's control had snapped just as hard as mine, and he was on a mission to make me scream now.

Cool water leaked out everywhere, soaking the sheets, but I was already lost to my climax as Kody fucked me hard enough to make the headboard slam against the wall.

His mouth found mine, muffling my screams as I found my release. And again. Holy shit. Then he sat up slightly, changing our position and pausing ever so briefly.

I was still shaking through the tail end of my climax, but I held still as he spread my pussy with his fingers. His dick was still buried inside me, but he was going for my clit. A second later, heat scorched through me, wax dripping directly onto that tight bundle of nerves.

To say I shattered would be an understatement. Kody gripped my hip, pumping harder as he chased his own orgasm, filling my cunt with his hot load while I moaned and thrashed and tugged on my restraints.

Oh yeah. Temperature play was *fun*. And I was going to bet we were far from done for the night, too.

I loved my life.

10

STEELE

rch and I let Kody have his alone time with MK for the night... It seemed like the decent thing to do, seeing as it *was* their wedding night. But shit, I wasn't a damn saint. So when Kody slipped out of the bedroom in the morning to go make our girl some coffee, I was lurking in the hallway pretending to admire one of Carolyn's paintings.

The second Kody disappeared toward the kitchen—shooting me a knowing eye roll—I slipped into the bedroom and locked the door. *Hah, take that Archer.*

My Hellcat was still fast asleep, all beautifully tussled in a mess of sheets and bare skin. Goddamn, she was like an angel when she slept... then she'd wake up and turn into a fiery vixen.

As quietly as I could, I climbed into the bed Kody had just recently vacated, and she gravitated into my embrace like a magnet.

"Max," she murmured with a contented sigh. "Love you."

I smiled so hard it hurt my cheeks. I'd never get sick of that. "I love you too, Hellcat."

She snuggled tighter into my side, the sheet slipping from her body to reveal the smooth skin of her bare hip. Crap, now I had a boner.

"What are we doing today?" she mumbled, her face against my chest.

I pressed my lips to her hair, tightening my arms around her. She fit against me like my other half. Like my missing piece. "I was thinking we could just stay here in bed for a while." Because there was nowhere I'd rather be than beside her.

"Mmmm, did you?" she replied with a yawn, tilting her face back to blink up at me sleepily. "And would we be sleeping?"

I wet my lips. "Are you tired?"

She gave a sleepy laugh. "Exhausted. But I don't wanna sleep anymore." To prove her point, she slid up the bed and kissed me softly on the lips. Then again. Then I couldn't help myself, I slid my hand into her hair and crushed my mouth to hers, kissing her desperately like I'd been wanting to do all damn night.

"Much better than sleeping," she whispered as my lips moved to her neck and my hand trailed down her bare side.

Humming my agreement, I danced my fingers over her hip and dipped them between her legs. The evidence of predawn fun with Kody was clear, but that didn't deter me—especially not when she gave a little whimper and pushed against my hand. Holy hell, I loved when she made that noise. It made me feel like a fucking god.

"I actually wanted to ask you something," I admitted as I slid two fingers inside her pussy and located her clit with my thumb. It was probably a bit sly to ask her an important question while I was finger-blasting her, but... whatever. It was our most comfortable state.

Her breath caught with a moan as I pumped my hand, stroking along her inner walls in search of that elusive G-spot. "Anything," she panted.

I grinned, then kissed her hard, tugging on her lower lip with my teeth before releasing. Fuck it, now or never, Max. Spit it out. "Will you marry me too?"

MK stilled, so I did too.

"Seriously?" she asked.

I frowned. "Um... yeah?" I'd sort of assumed that was in the cards, but... had I missed my opportunity?

She wrinkled her nose, frowning back at me. "Of course I will. I can't believe you even had to ask."

Relief washed over me, and I smiled. "Phew. Okay. Cool. Good chat."

One of her brows dipped. "Good chat? Max… you're halfway through getting me off and just asked me to marry you. That's…" She trailed off with a laugh. "Yeah, fair enough. Good chat."

Smiling, she cupped her hands on either side of my face and kissed me hard, her tongue toying with my lip piercing in a way that made me think of how her tongue teased my *other* piercings.

I took her hint, though, and started pumping my fingers back into her again. Then her phone started ringing beside the bed.

"Ignore it," she muttered against my lips, her hips rolling as she urged me to finger-fuck her harder.

"Yes, ma'am," I agreed, giving her what she wanted while using my thumb on her clit.

The ringing stopped, then immediately started again as she moaned and clawed at the back of my neck.

"Don't stop," she gasped, rocking harder on my hand. "Don't…"

She was close, I could feel it in the way her pussy clenched my fingers and in the way her legs shook with tiny trembles. And her phone rang *again*.

"Someone *really* wants to talk to you, beautiful," I muttered with a laugh as she gasped and thrashed on my hand.

"Shut up," she groaned, writhing under my touch. "That's what voicemail is for. Fuck, Max, I'm so close…"

I leaned in and claimed her lips with my own, kissing her hard and swallowing her moans as she climaxed. My thumb continued rubbing circles over her swollen clit and her pussy while she shuddered and moaned into my kiss. Making MK come was easily my favorite pastime, even if my dick was so hard I was two seconds away from coming in my pants like a teenager.

Her phone rang *again,* and I reluctantly rolled away. "You'd better answer that," I told her with a husky laugh. "Seems important."

She mumbled a curse, her chest heaving and her cheeks flushed. But she still wriggled across the bed to swipe her phone from the bedside table.

"Get that dick out, Max Steele," she ordered. "I want it in my mouth the second this call is over."

I grinned and tugged my sweats down obediently as she watched, her phone almost forgotten in her hand as her hungry eyes locked on my multi-pierced erection. I gripped it firmly, running my thumb down the ladder rungs, and gave a soft groan as she watched... Then her phone rang again.

"Shit," she muttered, glancing down. Then a frown creased her brow. "It's Monica."

I froze, dick still in hand, and she cast a worried look at me before bringing the phone to her ear.

"Monica? Sorry I missed your—" She broke off, listening to her company's CEO, then her eyes widened in shock. Shit, that couldn't be good.

Wincing, I tucked my dick back into my pants and sat up to pay attention as MK blinked and ran a hand through her hair.

"Holy shit," she exclaimed a moment later. "Yeah, okay. Yeah, we can leave today if there's a flight. Do you have any idea how—" She broke off again, probably because Monica was already answering that question. MK grimaced and shook her head. "Right. I see. Okay, I'll... Yeah, actually, if you could sort that out, it'd be a huge help. I'll let the guys know, and we will head back into Tokyo."

Crap. That definitely wasn't good.

Not waiting for her to end the call, I slid out of bed and pulled our suitcases from the closet to start packing. I didn't need to know what the situation was, only that it sounded urgent.

"Thank you for calling me, Monica," my girl told her CEO with a sigh. "I'll see you soon."

I glanced over my shoulder to see her ending the call and raised a brow in question.

She tossed her phone onto the blankets, then looked up at me with dread and worry painted all over her face. "We need to go to Pretoria," she informed me, despite me having already guessed as much.

I nodded, crossing to the door, and unlocked it. I jerked it open and bellowed for Kody and Archer, then turned back to MK, where she still sat in shock in the middle of the bed. She was still naked, her hair in a mess of waves around her shoulders.

"What's happened?" I came back to the bed and sat to take her hands in mine.

She blinked at me again, then gave a small headshake. "Someone broke into the Brilliance vault," she told me with an edge of disbelief.

Confusion rippled through me, and I tilted my head to the side. "That... sucks, but why can't Monica handle it? She's the Wittenberg CEO, and surely, diamond thefts are just a part of the business." I didn't understand why MK, who was the owner but not involved in the running of the company, needed to be brought in to handle it.

She shook her head again, just as Archer and Kody burst into the room with panic all over their faces. "No, not any vault, *the* vault. The original Brilliance vault. And they didn't just steal a bunch diamonds... they only took one. The Wittenberg Diamond."

Stunned shock hit us all, then Kody perfectly summarized what we were all thinking.

"Fuck," he murmured.

The Wittenberg Diamond was a ninety-six carat, fancy pink, princess-cut diamond that had been stored in one of the most secure private vaults on earth. How the fuck someone managed to break into *that*... it blew my damn mind.

I scrubbed a hand over my face, then tipped my head to the suitcases I'd started packing. "Arch, get packing. Kody, let your mom know we're leaving today."

For once, they just did as I told them without argument. Meanwhile, I gave MK's hand a gentle tug. "You wanna take a shower? They're capable of packing us up."

She flashed me a knowing grin before glancing down at her state of undress. I had no doubt in my mind that Kody had wiggled in a pre-dawn quickie before I'd woken her up, too.

"Probably a good idea," she agreed, climbing out of the bed totally unashamed of her nudity.

I grabbed our towels and clean clothes, and Archer grabbed her around the waist when she crossed over to say good morning to him. A minute later, I needed to clear my throat to make him release our girl, and he shot me a glare as MK took my hand on the way to the shower.

Sucker. Hellcat was nothing if not an impeccable multitasker, and there was no reason why she couldn't get clean *and* dirty all at the same time.

MADISON KATE

It was a full day and night of travel to get to Pretoria from Tokyo, but it was made a whole hell of a lot less taxing by the use of a private jet that Monica's assistant had arranged for us in Japan. The company had their own planes, of course, but it was quicker to hire one that was already in the right airport.

When we landed in Johannesburg, I was dead on my feet. I'd barely slept on the flight from Tokyo, partly from stress and partly because the boys had wanted to take full advantage of being on a private plane. Not that I was complaining. Orgasms helped calm me down, and they all knew it.

A driver was waiting for us after we'd cleared customs, as

expected, and an hour later we were checking into our hotel. Monica had left a message during our flight to let me know the situation was no longer urgent—whatever that meant—and that she'd see me the next morning.

Nervous energy prevented me from sleeping well, though. Even after Archer gave it his best effort to exhaust me, I was still keyed up and anxious. Someone had stolen a priceless diamond from a supposedly impenetrable vault. The why seemed fairly obvious: It was fucking priceless. But I couldn't wrap my brain around the who or the how.

Also nagging at my mind was why nothing *else* had been taken. That vault contained the value of that diamond several times over in other stones, yet only *one* had been taken. That struck me as odd. Surely if it was a greed theft, they'd have taken a whole lot more than one diamond... no matter how valuable that one was.

Somewhere around dawn I gave up trying to sleep and went to shower and get dressed for the day. I'd had several meetings with Monica here in Pretoria back when I took control of my inheritance and appointed her as CEO of Wittenberg, but I hadn't been back to our headquarters in over a year. Truthfully, I'd felt like an imposter the last time I'd met with Monica there. It wasn't a comfortable feeling. Afterward, I'd made a point of meeting her at her home or my hotel, on the few occasions I'd visited in person.

"Ready to go?" Steele asked when I emerged from the bathroom. He had a to-go coffee ready for me. He must have gone out to get it while I was dressing. Thoughtful bastard.

I gave him a tight smile and accepted the coffee. "Do I look okay?"

His gaze traveled down my body, heated and appreciative. I'd probably leaned too hard on the corporate look in a desperate attempt to look like I *belonged* at the billion-dollar company headquarters. It was just lucky I had enough clothing options in my luggage to pull together a cohesive outfit.

"You look fucking smoking hot," he replied with a slow grin, "but did you have to go with pants? How am I supposed to feel you up on the drive over in those?"

I flashed him a hard look, smoothing my sweaty palms down the front of my tailored black trousers. They ended an inch above my ankle, showing off the classic black Louboutin shoes that I'd added to my "boss bitch" wardrobe after seeing Hades wear them so often.

"You're *not*," I muttered. "I don't need to turn up with messy hair and smudged lipstick today, Max Steele. Keep that dick tucked away until we're done at Wittenberg."

He chuckled, holding the door open for me. "Spoilsport."

I rolled my eyes, knowing full well I'd just challenged him. "Where are Kody and Arch?"

"Went ahead." He closed the door after us and placed a hand on the small of my back as we headed for the elevators. "Arch was paranoid, muttering about it being an ambush to kill you or something. You know what he's like."

I smiled. I did know, and I loved him for it. Archer took "protective" to a whole other level, but as it'd kept me alive in the past, I'd learned not to argue.

Steele stole a couple of kisses in the elevator on the way down to the foyer but kept them light enough to not mess up my lipstick. Sneaky shit. Once in the back of the limo with the privacy screen firmly in place, he proved that pants really weren't a deterrent when he was determined.

By the time our car pulled up at Wittenberg, my cheeks were flushed and I couldn't wipe the smile from my face. I was also a hell of a lot calmer and less nervous. When I strolled into the impressive foyer of the South African Reserve Bank with my sexy man on my arm, it was with boss-level confidence.

Wittenberg, and Brilliance, owned two floors of the monolithic, dark skyscraper, so it was even more inconceivable that someone had robbed our vault. It was literally inside a bank.

There were layers upon layers of security to even get into the elevator, which was only a good thing for a diamond company. But it also meant that by the time we'd reached the forty-eighth floor, where Monica's office was, I was jittery again.

"I need to pee," I muttered under my breath as we stepped out of the elevator. There was a restroom just a short way down the hall from the elevators, so I left Steele at the reception desk and continued on to the ladies' room. Nervous peeing was a real thing.

When I was done, I washed my hands and fixed my makeup—thanks Steele—then made my way back out to the reception area. The young woman who'd been there a few minutes ago was gone, likely taking Steele to wherever Kody and Archer were already waiting. I didn't want to go barging my ass in like I owned the place—even if I did—so I took a seat and waited patiently for her to return.

A moment later, an expensively suited man in his fifties came stalking through the foyer and paused when he saw me sitting there. It wasn't even subtle, either, the way he stopped mid-stride and raked his gaze over me from head to toe. Then a slimy smile creased his lips.

"Hello, beautiful," he purred, coming closer and extending a hand. "I'm Friedrich Nkosi. You're early; I think I like you already."

I narrowed my eyes at him in a squint, ignoring his extended hand. Clearing my throat, I stood from my seat so he was no longer looking down on me and smoothed my hands down my pants.

"Friedrich," I said in a cool voice. "I don't think we've met. My name isn't *beautiful*, though. It's—"

"You will call me Mr. Nkosi, girl," he snapped, a cruel glint in his eye before his gaze dipped obviously to my cleavage, "or your first day as my intern will be *rather* unpleasant." The smile on his lips suggested that he'd enjoy making it unpleasant.

Gross.

I drew a breath, pushing aside my urge to throat-punch this prick. Instead, I pasted a frosty smile on my face and tried again. "As I was saying before you decided to threaten me, *Friedrich*, my name is Madison Kate, not *beautiful*. Is this how you introduce yourself to all women? If so, I'm appalled."

He sneered at me, full of outrage that I'd spoken back. "You listen here, you mouthy little bitch—" As he spoke, he grabbed my wrist like he planned to drag me somewhere with him.

Bad move, buddy.

No sooner had he yanked on my wrist than a tattooed fist flew at his face and he crashed to the floor with a howl of pain.

"You touch her again, and I'll kill you," Archer snarled at the slimy suit.

I couldn't stop myself from grinning up at him. I hadn't even seen him approach, but my focus had been on the creeper who clearly enjoyed sexually assaulting his interns.

"What the fuck?" the man on the floor screamed. "Who the fuck—"

"Ms. Wittenberg!" a woman exclaimed, cutting off the man's outraged yells. I tipped my head to peer past Archer and found a gorgeous dark-skinned woman in head-to-toe Prada hurrying toward us. "I am *so* sorry. My goodness, are you okay?"

"Is *she* okay?" the man snarled. "That bastard just punched me in the face! I'm bleeding! Call security!"

Monica van Wyk—Wittenberg CEO—shot a scathing look at

him in return. "Are you fucking deaf, Friedrich? *Ms. Wittenberg* is here for a meeting with me. Her *husband* must have taken offense to something you said or did, so if we're calling security for anyone, it's you."

Finally, my name must have sunk through his Neanderthal brain, and the man paled beneath the hand he held over his bloody nose. His gaze whipped back to mine, and I gave him a cool smile.

"Friedrich, I think it's probably best if you pack up your desk, don't you?" I narrowed my eyes and leaned into Archer as his arm circled my waist. "If that's how you treat your interns, or any woman, then there is no place for you in my company."

He blinked up at me in total shock, then shifted his gaze back to Monica in dismay.

My CEO just shrugged and spread her hands wide. "You heard her, Friedrich. You're fired. I'll have security escort you out."

Monica held out an arm to me, ushering me through the foyer in the direction of her office, and we left Friedrich behind, bellowing his outrage as the receptionist placed a call to security. Being that the Wittenberg office was inside a bank-owned building, there were security guards lurking *everywhere*. They'd take care of things.

The whole office floor seemed to watch me as Monica led the way to her corner office, and I hurried to follow her and escape the scrutiny. Not *exactly* the impression I wanted to leave as the company owner, but that prick did *not* deserve to keep his job.

Monica closed the door behind us, and I spotted Kody and

Steele already seated on her leather sofa.

"Madison Kate, I am so extremely sorry about Friedrich. Whatever he said—"

"He grabbed her wrist," Archer growled, looking a whole lot like he wanted to go back and grind Friedrich Nkosi into the floor.

Monica's brows hitched, and a wince tightened her eyes. "I can't apologize enough," she continued, addressing me directly as she motioned to some vacant seats. "But is it bad that you did me a favor? We've known he has been abusing interns for far too long, but none of the girls have been willing to give any evidence or... anything that could support firing him. So, thank you."

I grinned, sitting down as the hot rush of adrenaline faded away. "You're welcome. Want me to antagonize anyone else that you need to get rid of?"

Monica smiled but shook her head. "Somehow I doubt you did much to antagonize Friedrich." She sighed, then sat down herself. "Now. I asked you here because of the Wittenberg Diamond theft."

I nodded. "You did. But it no longer is urgent?"

She pursed her perfectly painted lips. "That's correct."

Leaning forward with his elbows on his knees, Archer growled an irritated sound beside me. "Forgive my bluntness," he muttered, sounding anything but apologetic, "but how is the theft of an almost billion-dollar jewel no longer urgent?"

Monica wrinkled her nose and gave a small sigh. "Because it's no longer missing."

12

ARCHER

y knuckles didn't even hurt from decking that creep. When I'd seen him leering at my girl as I approached, it'd been damn hard to refrain from killing him with my bare hands. Then when he grabbed her... Yeah, I saw red. Prick.

"Wait, what do you mean?" Kate asked, shaking her head in confusion. "It wasn't stolen?"

"Kind of a big fuck up if it was just misplaced, don't you think?" Kody murmured with a quirked brow.

Monica shook her head. "It wasn't misplaced... I tell you, this whole thing is the strangest thing I've seen in my whole life. Can I, perhaps, show you the vault? Madison Kate, I know you've been down there once before."

Nodding quickly, Kate unfolded her legs and stood. "Absolutely, yes. I need to visualize this whole thing better anyway."

Monica led the way back out to the elevators, chatting with Kate as we walked, but I wasn't paying attention. Truthfully, I didn't give a fuck about the missing diamond. Between the four of us, we had enough money to live like royalty for several lifetimes over. We didn't *need* priceless diamonds. My concern was that this was somehow an attack on *her*.

Could someone have stolen this jewel to lure her back to Pretoria? Who stood to gain if my wife was murdered, though? Per the somewhat illegal and highly deceitful prenup that her father had signed on her behalf, everything she owned would pass to me in the event of her death, not to any other surviving heirs of Abel Wittenberg.

Could it be linked back to the trouble in Shadow Grove? Hades was dealing with a shit-fight that was partly our responsibility. Honestly, I was surprised Chase hadn't already taken any swipes at us. His revenge plans seemed to be laser-focused on Hades for now, though—unsurprising, given what I knew of the psychopath from his first life. He'd been obsessed with owning her back then, and it seemed to have only got worse since she'd burned his entire family and their empire to ash.

I'd been so sure this was a trap I'd convinced Kody to come

over early with me to check. How the fuck there could be an attack inside such a secure building, I didn't know. Then again, *someone* had broken into the vault. Anything was possible.

With a heavy sigh, I scrubbed a hand over my beard and tried to refocus on the conversation between Kate and Monica. She'd been studying so hard to understand the inner workings of her company, but with the sheer scale of Wittenberg and Brilliance, it would be a long time yet before she'd be comfortable taking over.

Monica seemed like a good CEO until then, though. It helped that one of the top mercenaries in the Guild had personally headhunted her for the job, poaching her from a competitor with an offer of double the salary.

"How's your hand?" Monica asked me as the elevator descended to the basement of the high-rise. "Do you need ice or anything?"

Kody snickered. "And not the type in the vaults."

I gave him a flat glare back—he was nowhere near as funny as he thought—and shook my head. "Nah, I barely even tapped that slimy fuck."

Monica gave me a long look, but Kate just looked... *fuck*. She looked turned on as hell. Unable to help myself, I met her heated gaze and flexed my fist to make the joints crack. Such a minx— her breath caught, and her tongue swiped over her lips.

Steele jabbed an elbow into my ribs, breaking my eye contact with Kate.

"Cut it out," he muttered to me, scolding. I just shot him a smirk back.

The elevator door opened on the vault floor, and Monica took the lead again. There were several security checkpoints before we got through to the Brilliance vault, then we were standing inside a small room lined with drawers. Of the four of us, only Kate had visited the vault before, but I knew from her description that the drawers were all velvet-lined and contained all of the rarest jewels found in the Brilliance mines.

"This is where the Wittenberg Diamond was stored," Monica told us, pulling out a key and unlocking one of the larger drawers. She pulled it open and showed us the empty interior with a perfectly molded velvet lining where the diamond had sat for decades. "And you saw how much security we needed to pass through to access this vault. The idea that someone broke in here is... It's simply unbelievable."

I scowled, looking around the vault. She was right.

"Could it have been an inside job?" Steele asked, voicing my own thoughts.

"That was our first line of investigation," Monica replied, nodding, "but no. I don't believe that's what happened. The gaps in security footage, the tampering with the alarm systems, the evidence of actual safecracking techniques... this was done by a professional."

"You sound like you have some ideas," Kate commented, her

sharp gaze on Monica's face.

The older woman just gave a small incline of her head and indicated for us to exit the vault. "If you've seen enough, we can speak further back upstairs. There's someone I'd like you to meet as well."

No one spoke as Monica went through the process of securing the vault behind us, and I noticed the focused way Kate watched every movement. She was trying to work out how the hell someone could have broken in, as we all were.

Monica gave her a knowing smile, and both their heels clicked on the concrete floor as they led the way back through the security checkpoints. Some of them were manned with actual human guards, some were electronic, requiring biometric scans or codes keyed in. In short... the Brilliance vault was impenetrable. Until now, apparently.

"Are there guards down here around the clock?" Kody asked as we waited for the elevator once more.

Monica shook her head. "Only during business hours. That's why there are so many additional security measures. But remember, we're inside the reserve bank building. To even attempt this robbery, you'd need to first get *down* to this floor."

I grunted. She had a point. It wasn't exactly a simple task to get into the building, even during business hours with a legitimate reason to be here.

My mind wandered again as the elevator made multiple stops

on the way back up to Monica's floor. People got on and off, preventing any substantial conversation, and I ran the facts of the robbery through my head. The complexity of the job, the targeted item, the value involved with the risk... South Africa wasn't exactly the kindest court system on criminals, either.

The most important point, though, was what Monica had said before we went down to the vault. The diamond was no longer missing. So either it'd been *returned*—which seemed unlikely, considering the drawer had been empty—or they had already worked out who had it and where it was.

Maybe she wanted us to get it back? But Brilliance had their own shady connections to accomplish a job like that. She wouldn't need to involve Kate.

Vaguely in the back of my mind, something was whispering at me. Like I'd heard about a similar theft somewhere else along the way.

Back up on the Wittenberg floor, everything seemed calm, with Friedrich the handsy fuck having already been removed by security. Monica directed us into the boardroom instead of her office this time and put in an order with her assistant for coffees to be brought in.

"Madison Kate," she started with a tight smile when the boardroom door was closed. "Forgive me for asking this, but you never knew your grandparents, is that correct?"

My wife shook her head, a small frown creasing her brow. My

fingers itched to smooth it away, but I tightened my grip on the arms of the chair to stop myself. Not the time or the place, dude.

"I never met my grandfather," she confirmed, "and my memories of my grandmother are... patchy." She winced slightly at that, and my chest tightened. Even after almost two years of regular therapy, she hadn't recovered more than a few spotty memories of her childhood. The trauma of watching her mother be murdered had just wiped whole sections of her past away.

Monica nodded. "Yes, I thought so. When I was making the decision to come here and run your company, I spent some time speaking with the members of the board, particularly the older ones who'd had personal interactions with Abel before his death. I wanted to understand what kind of foundation this company had before committing myself." She paused, smoothing a hand over her neatly sprayed updo. "I'm sure it comes as no great shock that a lot of diamond mines built their worth on theft, violence, and murder. Brilliance seemed one of the few exceptions."

"Seemed?" Kate echoed, her eyes wide in alarm.

Monica gave a small nod but didn't respond immediately. A moment later, her assistant came back in with a tray of coffees, and we waited patiently while the young woman served out drinks to us all.

"I've got the feeling you know who broke into your vault," Steele commented when we were alone again. "Is this connected to Abel's business practices?"

Monica pursed her lips, thoughtful. "I believe so," she murmured. "The thief... I am only speculating, of course. But based on what I know of this break in, along with some incidents with my previous employer and the information law enforcement has shared with me? Yes, I think I know who stole the Wittenberg Diamond."

It took me a moment to remember who Monica had worked for before Wittenberg. But when the pieces clicked together, I gave a low groan and scrubbed a hand over my short beard.

"You know?" she asked me with a raised brow.

I jerked a nod. "It fits the profile. And you said the diamond is no longer missing? Let me guess. It's been returned to someone with a stronger claim of ownership than Brilliance."

Her smile was brittle. "Indeed."

Kate's confused gaze darted between the two of us, her brow furrowed. "Okay, someone fill in the blanks."

I blew out a heavy sigh. It all made sense now; there was only one thief I'd ever heard of who could break into a vault like Brilliance's. "This wasn't any ordinary jewel thief. This was Hermes."

13

MADISON KATE

I met Archer's pale blue eyes, still waiting for the rest of the explanation. Because that statement meant nothing to me.

"Uh, like... the Greek god with flying shoes?" Kody asked, echoing my thoughts perfectly. We were so on the same wavelength sometimes.

Archer gave a small eye roll. "Like the Greek god of *thieves* and *trickery*," he corrected. "It's just a nickname because no one actually knows who Hermes is. Hell, I don't even know where the name came from, I just heard him—or her—mentioned by Phillip when I was a kid. Remember when the Monet was stolen?" He tipped his head to the side, asking Kody and Steele.

Kody scratched the bridge of his nose, looking confused, but Max nodded.

"I overheard Phillip discussing it a few weeks later. Hermes was mentioned as the most likely culprit due to the painting's less-than-legal purchase conditions." Archer grimaced. "You know what old Percy D'Ath was like. The more illegal, the better for that old bastard."

Understanding had me nodding. Archer's *great*-grandfather had been deep into illegal activities. So it was no shock he had a stolen Monet painting in his house.

"Well," Monica continued, still speaking to me directly. I liked that about her. She didn't talk to Archer first, like so many other people did. Simply because he oozed big dick energy didn't mean he was in charge. "Once I put two and two together, I could see Hermes's fingerprints all over this, which is why I wanted you to come here in person. The diamond has been located because a young woman tried to return it to us yesterday afternoon."

My lips parted in shock. "She... tried to *return* it? That seems..."

"Very strange?" Monica finished with a laugh when I trailed off. "I agree. But nonetheless, she did. She claims that when she came home from work there was a gift-wrapped box on her kitchen counter. Inside... the Wittenberg Diamond. She immediately packed her kids into the car and drove here to return it."

Holy shit. "She brought her kids?" I don't know why that mattered. It just did.

Monica smiled. "Yes. I put them up in one of our corporate apartments for the night because your flight was still hours away from landing and her children are young. But I felt quite strongly that you would want to meet her yourself, once you understood her story."

I felt like fucking Alice tumbling down a rabbit hole. "Don't keep me in suspense, Monica." I said it jokingly, but there was an edge of concern in my tone that Steele must have heard. His hand found my knee and gave me a squeeze of reassurance.

"Amahle Dlamini is her name. She comes from Refilwe, which was originally a miners' village. Her family originally owned the land that the Brilliance mine now sits on. Your grandfather, as a very young man, purchased the land from Amahle's great-grandparents. But when he struck the deal, he had no money of his own to buy it with. So he came to an agreement—signed contracts and everything—with Amahle's great-grandfather to essentially *rent* the land for a period of time. Then twelve months later, it was formally purchased with payment in the form of several diamonds found in the new mine." She gave me a pointed look, and a heavy sigh escaped my chest.

"Fuck," I whispered.

Monica gave a small nod. "My thoughts exactly."

"I'm lost," Kody admitted. "What does that have to do with the Wittenberg Diamond being stol—" He cut himself off as understanding dawned. "Oh."

"Idiot," Archer muttered, and Kody flipped him off.

"How did the diamond end up back in Wittenberg's metaphorical crown if it was used to purchase the land?" I asked, desperate to hear the rest of the story. The growing dread in my belly said I already knew the answer, though. Fucking hell.

Monica cleared her throat and sipped her coffee. "Amahle's great-grandfather had a drinking problem. Unfortunately, he also had a bragging problem and told a few too many people about the diamonds Abel had paid him with. So when his house was broken into and the diamonds stolen"—she shrugged and shook her head—"no one was surprised. It was assumed that someone he ran his mouth to under the influence had just seen an easy mark and acted on it. Now, though... it seems a little more sinister."

Steele gave my knee a reassuring squeeze, and I rubbed the bridge of my nose. I had a headache building, that was for fucking sure.

"Okay." I drew a deep breath, then exhaled heavily. "So Abel paid for the land with diamonds, one of which we are assuming was one enormous pink diamond, which then went missing... and somehow that one turned up back in the Brilliance vault as the Wittenberg Diamond? Are we sure they're one and the same? Could there have been two?"

"Nothing is impossible," Monica replied with a shrug. "The one given to Ms. Dlamini's family was uncut and unpolished. There's no real way to know for sure, given that everyone involved in those deals are now dead. The only part that makes me believe her is Hermes's involvement."

I frowned. "That's proof? He—or she—is a thief. How would they know the truth?"

"Not proof," Archer rumbled, "but as close to. The coincidences seem suspicious enough even without Hermes's involvement. What are the odds of *two* pink diamonds of over one hundred carats being found in the same mine within a short time period? Especially when one goes missing..." He quirked a brow at me. "Sounds a whole lot like old Abel decided to retrieve it and set it all up to look like a common robbery."

"I had one of the security teams do some digging through the archives last night," Monica added. "The diamond given to the Dlamini family was estimated at one hundred and thirty carats. The earliest record of the Wittenberg Diamond was six months *after* Mr. Dlamini reported his as being stolen. The raw weight was never recorded; the first documentation was after cutting and polishing."

Kody gave a low whistle, shaking his head. "Abel was a dirty cheat, huh?"

"Sure seems that way," I agreed softly. I bit my lower lip, thinking. "So what do we do? Is there any way of knowing the truth?"

My CEO gave a small headshake. "Technically, Ms. Dlamini has no legal claim over the diamond. There's no concrete evidence that it's the stone stolen from her family."

"But we know better," I whispered, and Monica nodded.

"It's your call, Madison Kate. This is your family's company, and ultimately, the diamond belongs to you. Ms. Dlamini isn't trying to keep it, either. She came here to return it, terrified she would be charged with the theft."

Archer leaned forward with his elbows on the table. "How'd she know where to bring it?"

Steele scoffed. "Wouldn't be a hard guess, bro. Huge-ass diamond shows up, you're probably going to take it to the one and only diamond mine in the area."

"Fair point," Archer agreed.

I frowned. "So, you're saying we can take the diamond back and be done with it all," I said, wanting to be clear on the options Monica was suggesting. "Or we can rectify the sins of my forefathers and return the diamond to Ms. Dlamini."

No one responded to that, and the silence was thick enough to touch.

"Fucking hell," I murmured.

"Would you like to meet her before making that decision?" Monica offered.

I nodded quickly. "I think so, yes."

Archer's brows shot up, like he disagreed, but Monica was focused on me and probably didn't see him.

"I thought you might. Wait here; I had her come in this morning." My CEO gracefully unfolded from her chair and left the room.

When the door closed behind her, my guys all turned to me with varying looks of concern etched across their features.

"This feels like a setup," Archer growled.

I rolled my eyes. "How? You think she's going to come back with a grenade launcher or some shit? Not everything is a death threat, Sunshine.

He scowled back at me. "You sure about that, Princess?"

"Sure enough," I snapped. "Monica isn't setting me up. I trust her. She wouldn't be running my damn company if I didn't."

"Okay, what about this woman who *found* the diamond," Steele redirected. "She could be a con artist. She could be Hermes, for all we know."

Kody snorted a laugh. "That seems improbable. Hermes took the diamond and was free and clear with no trace. Why come back at all? Nah, that's stupid. This chick could have said nothing and kept it, but she didn't."

"I agree." I nodded firmly. "She had *zero* obligation to return it, but she didn't even hesitate to do the right thing. Why are we?"

None of them had a response to that, and silence reigned for a moment.

"Unless that was what she wanted you to think," Archer muttered eventually. "It'd be hard to sell a stolen diamond of that size without attracting attention."

I sighed heavily, glaring back at him. "It would. But if someone were skilled enough to break into the Brilliance vault, don't you think they'd already have the contacts necessary to make that sale? There would be *absolutely* no need to come back here and offer to hand it back on the off chance that you were allowed to keep it. That's moronic, Sunshine."

"I'm with MK on this," Kody announced. "Besides, from what you just said about Hermes, their whole gig is returning stolen items to their rightful owners. Which, by that logic, clears this woman of suspicion."

"I'm sure Hermes does plenty of theft for personal gain too," Steele commented, thoughtful, "but I'm inclined to agree on this one. But are you seriously thinking about just *giving away* the Wittenberg Diamond?" He gave me a look like I'd grown a tail.

I tipped my head to the side, meeting his eyes. "No." He let out a heavy breath, and I amended my statement. "I can't give away something that was never supposed to be mine in the first place. And it sure as shit sounds like the Wittenberg Diamond was never mine. So, no... I'm thinking about *returning stolen property*."

Steele's brows went high, but he gave a slow nod. It was only natural, I guess, to question someone's sanity when they were so casual about giving up such a valuable jewel. But to put it bluntly, I didn't need the money. My company didn't need the money. But good karma? Well... that was something we could all use a little more of.

The door opened then, cutting off any further conversation,

and Monica entered with a young woman following behind. She looked younger than me and was *heavily* pregnant. A toddler sat on her hip, cuddling into her side, and another child held onto her brightly patterned skirt as they entered the boardroom.

Monica invited them to sit down, and the woman gave her a grateful smile as she arranged herself with the toddler still balanced on her lap. The older child climbed up into the seat beside her and peered across at Kody with huge eyes.

"Amahle this is Madison Kate Wittenberg." Monica introduced us in a warm, calming tone. "She only recently inherited the company." The implication behind that statement suggested Monica was telling Amahle that, although I shared Abel's surname, I wasn't him.

"It's nice to meet you, ma'am," the woman greeted me with a nervous smile. "I understand you traveled a long way; I hope the flight was pleasant."

I smiled back at her. "It was, thank you." Unable to ignore the way the toddler stared at me, I shifted my attention to the small person. "Hello."

The little girl flashed a smile, then buried her face in her mother's dress. Amahle chuckled and rubbed the toddler's back. "This is Retha," she told me, "and Esmarie." She indicated to the older girl, who was now making faces at Kody. A quick glance told me he was making them back at her. Fucking Kody was so good with kids.

"Monica told me that you found the Wittenberg Diamond in your home yesterday?" I started, keeping my voice and my expression as friendly and nonthreatening as possible. I could see the lines of tension around her eyes, and her hand trembled slightly as she patted Retha's back. She was scared.

Amahle gave a jerking nod. "Yes, ma'am. When I saw what it was, I knew it had come from here."

"Why didn't you call the police?" Archer asked, his voice a low rumble that caused Amahle's eyes to widen.

Still, she held firm and tilted her chin up. "Because the police are not all good men, and there was a high chance the diamond would never be returned to you. I acted on instinct and came straight here. I didn't even tell anyone where I was going."

I hated that so much of law enforcement all around the world was blackened with corruption. But it didn't surprise me, considering my own uncle had been a member of the Shadow Grove Police Department while he'd stalked my mother and then me.

"You live alone?" I asked, simply out of curiosity.

Amahle's attention shifted back to me, and she nodded. "Yes, my husband, unfortunately, passed four months ago. I have no siblings, and my parents died years ago. I'm the last of my family, and the only one who knew of the deal between my great-grandfather and Abel Wittenberg."

My chest tightened with sympathy for her. She was all alone

watching the way the light danced over the stone.

The door clicked as Monica re-entered, and I glanced up to meet her eyes. "Even without evidence beyond her story, I just feel like it's the truth. This diamond belongs to Ms. Dlamini and her little girls. But she was right when she said she had no use for it."

My CEO tilted her head to the side, questioning.

I looked back down at the diamond. It was mind-blowing to think so much money could be contained in a pretty pink rock smaller than my fist.

"Please arrange the value of the Wittenberg Diamond be paid out to Ms. Dlamini. She may not have any use for a diamond, but it's her property. So I'd like to buy it from her. Then, I think it would be in our best interest to have someone thoroughly investigate the circumstances around Wittenberg's ownership of the mine. Check the contracts, do all the digging necessary to find out how the fuck that diamond ended up back in our vault. There's every chance it was stolen by a random thief and sold. Then Abel could have bought it legally on the diamond market. But... if my grandfather stole it, then I want to know. If he did, if he even knew anything about it, then I want you to transfer a percentage of the Brilliance shares to Ms. Dlamini."

Monica beamed, her smile lighting up her face. "Absolutely, Ms. Wittenberg. I'll see it taken care of."

Kody sniffed dramatically, dabbing at his eyes with the edge of his T-shirt. "Is someone cutting onions in here?" he asked, blinking rapidly.

Steele smacked him in the back of the head. "Shut up, dickhead."

14

STEELE

Hellcat ended up spending the next few days in the office with Monica. Seeing as we were all still unwelcome in Shadow Grove—none of us wanted to risk Hades's wrath—it was the perfect time for MK to get a feel for everything her CEO did on a daily basis.

Having her so busy with work suited me just fine, though. When we'd mentioned hanging around for a while, Monica had suggested we visit the Wittenberg-owned private game reserve near Kruger—apparently one of the company's many, *many* fringe benefits. It played perfectly into my plans, though, and I spent the rest of the week working with Monica's executive assistant to put everything in place.

It required a few calls to Bree to get some details right, but in my defense, I didn't have my mom around to help me out with those decisions.

All in all, I was pretty pleased with myself when our car pulled up at the game reserve a week later. And a little nervous.

"Is this really necessary?" MK asked with a laugh as I tied a blindfold over her eyes before we got out of the vehicle.

"Probably not," I admitted, "but it's more fun. You trust me, right?"

Her lush lips curved in a grin. "With my whole life, Max Steele. But if this turns out to be a sex thing—"

Archer, pulling our luggage from the trunk, snorted a laugh. "If it's a sex thing, you'd be into it. Don't even play, Kate."

She chuckled but didn't deny it. Our girl was such a vixen; it was awesome. I loved how confident she was in her own sexuality, totally unafraid to ask for what she wanted in bed... or anywhere else, for that matter.

But this *wasn't* a sex thing—not yet, anyway—so I indicated for Kody and Archer to fuck right off. This was my moment. Mine and hers.

Kody flipped me off but grabbed some of the luggage. He and Archer followed one of the lodge staff and left us standing in front of the main entrance alone.

"We just going to stand here indefinitely?" she asked teasingly.

"Or are we waiting until we're alone so it can turn into a sex thing?"

I grinned, my hand on the small of her back because I couldn't *not* touch her. A blonde woman hurried out of the main lodge with an excited smile on her face and gave me a knowing nod.

"Hellcat, this is Julie. She's going to take you to freshen up." I indicated to Julie to keep the blindfold on my girl, and she gave me a nod of understanding.

"It's lovely to meet you, Ms. Wittenberg," Julie said in her friendly voice. "Would you mind if I took your hand? Just so you don't trip."

MK chuckled lightly. "Yeah, I probably don't want to trip. Nice to, uh, sort of meet you too, Julie. Max...?"

"Trust me, Hellcat," I replied, unable to fight the smile on my face.

She shrugged, and Julie led her away to a dressing room already set up and ready for her. Meanwhile, I hurried in the direction the guys had gone. It took me a few minutes to find them, then, when I entered the room, I wanted to smack them both.

"Guys, seriously? We have half an hour." I glared death as Archer poured an extra tumbler of whiskey and held it out to me.

Kody shrugged. "Yeah, but we need a bit of a Scotch buzz to control Archer's jealousy issues."

I grunted and took the glass from Arch. "Fair point." I gulped the liquor in one mouthful. "Now hurry the fuck up and get dressed. If either of you two screw this up for me, I'm supergluing your ass cheeks together."

"You sure Kate won't do that to you for this? You know she's not super fond of surprises." Arch gave me a sly smirk, like he'd quite enjoy her doing that to me. Asshole.

I ignored his teasing and grabbed my suit bag from the bed where one of them had left it. I was confident she would like *this* surprise. Surely.

"It'll be fine, bro," Kody assured me, gulping his own drink with a wince. "All girls like a surprise wedding that they had no input into. Right?"

I froze.

Fuck.

"Too late to back out now," Archer commented, *so* helpfully.

"You guys fucking suck," I muttered, stripping off my clothes and stalking into the bathroom to shower.

Their laughter followed me, and I rolled my eyes at their bullshit. I knew they were just joking, but damn, I was already so on edge worrying that Hellcat wouldn't like this... I didn't have the patience for teasing.

I showered quickly, then dressed in my black tuxedo and black shirt. A white shirt had looked way too prim and proper when I'd tried it on in the store. Back in the main bedroom, Arch and Kody were almost dressed, too, in similar tuxedos but with dark gray shirts instead.

"You two done with the jokes?" I scowled, smoothing my hands down my pants.

Kody smirked. "Not even close, bro."

Still, they kept the ribbing to a minimum while we headed down to the ballroom. It was beautifully decorated with soft pink flowers, and the floor-to-ceiling window looked out over the safari landscape. In about ten minutes, that window would display the sunset... hopefully, perfectly timed.

"You did well," Archer muttered quietly as we watched the lodge staff putting final touches on the decorations. "She'll love it."

Kody clapped me on the back. "You big softie, Max Steele."

I glared at him, but then it was time. We got into position, and I waited with bated breath as Julie led my still blindfolded bride into the room. She was like a damn goddess in a flowing, white silk gown. The lace details clung to her curves in a way that made my heart race and my dick hard, and I made a mental note to thank Bree later. Her choice was impeccable.

Julie looked over at us, her brows raised in question, and I gave a small nod in reply.

She said something quietly to MK, then carefully untied the loose blindfold. She would have had to remove it to do Hellcat's hair and makeup, but she'd promised to do it all without a mirror in the room so MK would have no clues about what was happening.

It wouldn't have been hard to guess, though.

My girl blinked a couple of times as the blindfold was

removed, then her eyes widened and I saw the sharp inhale of breath as she looked around. Then a second later, her eyes found me, and the smile on her face was bright enough to light up my whole damn world.

She ignored the bouquet of flowers that Julie was offering her, instead picking up her long skirt and running across the room toward us. She didn't even slow down when she drew close, launching herself into my arms and clinging to me tight.

I held her just as tight, adjusting my stance to take her weight, and breathed in her fresh scent. Thank fuck. She didn't seem mad.

"Max," she exclaimed, peeling herself away, and I reluctantly set her down. "You did all of this?"

I gave a small, uncomfortable shrug. "I had help."

"He did it all himself," Kody said. "Little romantic."

"I love it," she breathed, rising up on her toes to press her lush lips to mine. "I love *you*, Max Steele. This is incredible. How'd you organize it all so quick?"

I smiled and kissed her in response. But really, there wasn't much that was unachievable when you had the money to make it happen. The hardest part had been getting her dress measurements and arguing with Bree over whether she'd actually want a white dress or not. I'd said not, but Bree had argued that she wore lilac to marry Archer and red to marry Kody, so one of the three weddings needed a traditional white gown.

I was glad she'd won that one. Hellcat looked like something

VAULT

straight out of a dream.

Our civil celebrant cleared his throat softly, bringing our attention back to the reason we were all there, and I reluctantly released my girl. I supposed I could wait until we were married before kissing her again.

The ceremony was quick and to the point, none of the long-winded speeches about life and death, fidelity and all the other crap that normal weddings had. I barely heard a word of it, though. My whole focus was on my Hellcat. Archer even needed to prod me in the ribs when the celebrant wanted us to exchange rings.

"Shit," I whispered, feeling my cheeks heat slightly. "Sorry, I was..." *daydreaming about lifting those long white skirts up over my girl's waist and railing her from behind against that enormous window.*

"Here," Archer said in a gruff voice, handing me the ring I'd had made along with Kody's. We wanted our rings to fit perfectly with the one Archer had already given her so she could wear them together comfortably.

I fumbled a bit to slide her existing rings off first, then put all three back on in the order they'd been designed: mine on the bottom, Archer's in the middle, and Kody's on top. A complete set.

"Max," MK breathed, admiring her new ring, "it's gorgeous. You guys have had this planned for a while, huh?" Her smile said she wasn't at all mad about that fact, which was a relief.

"Actually, we had something extra made," I replied, reaching

135

into the pocket of my suit and pulling out the three identical black titanium rings I had stashed there. "You know... if you wanted to..."

She gasped when I uncurled my fingers to reveal the rings. Carefully, and with whispered words of love, she slid the first ring onto my finger, then turned to Kody and Archer to give them their matching rings.

"I don't know that this could have been any more perfect," she told me with shining eyes as she returned to me.

I grinned. "Oh, I can think of something."

Our celebrant pronounced us husband and wife, and I dipped her low as I kissed her hard. I didn't let up on kissing her until Kody poked me in the back, and I looked up to see my final surprise had arrived outside.

MK saw them a second later and gave a small squeal of excitement. "Lions at sunset? What the fuck, Max Steele? How? They're—"

"Big cats," I told her with a sly smirk. "For my Hellcat."

15

KODY

Whoever said the "honeymoon period" ever had to end was a moron. Or maybe they just needed to be in a poly relationship with their best friends and a woman who never seemed to sleep. Our stay at the Wittenberg game reserve was total bliss, then MK jumped at the chance to spend more time with Monica in her company's headquarters.

Eventually, though, the four of us agreed we needed to head back to the States to take care of our other businesses. I had my gyms to manage—although I'd been lucky to score some excellent staff to run them—and Arch had some less-than-legal businesses to check in on.

Steele put in a call to Zed to check whether we might be shot on site if we stepped back into Shadow Grove, but it seemed like Hades had bigger fish to fry than us.

"So... back to Shadow Grove, huh?" MK commented, standing beside me as we waited for her private jet to be ready for boarding. "Kinda feels weird to be going home."

I glanced down at her, looping my arm around her waist to pull her close. "I never left home, babe," I told her, channeling some of Steele's cheesy romantic shit. "My home is wherever you are."

A wide grin spread over her lips, and she chuckled. "Wow. Equally nauseating and adorable at the same time. I don't even know what to do with that."

"You love it; don't try and deny it, babe," I told her as I pulled her tighter and bent my neck to kiss her lips.

"Mmm," she hummed in reply. "I got a call from Monica this morning. Turns out, Abel never stole that diamond from Ahmale's great-grandfather. He purchased it already cut about eight months after the rock was stolen, our guys found all the paperwork verifying the sale. They're doing a bit more digging to trace it backwards but it's looking like Abel and Brilliance had nothing to do with the Dlamini family losing their diamond."

Wow. That was surprising but also a relief. From everything we'd learned of Abel Wittenberg, he didn't *seem* like that type of shady character. He and Katerina—MK's grandmother—had been decent people. At least according to anyone who'd known them.

"So… what are you going to do about those eighty-seven million dollars you paid Ahmale for the diamond?" I winced.

MK laughed and shook her head. "Nothing. In fact, I suggested to Monica that she still give Ahmale some Brilliance shares anyway." She shrugged and ruffled a hand through her hair. "So… do you think this plane has one of those big beds like the last one? It's a *long* flight back to Shadow Grove."

Fuck. My dick twitched just at that suggestion. There was something beyond awesome about group activities when MK was in the middle of it all, even when she threatened to bite my dick off if I high-fived Steele again. I knew she was bluffing; she totally loved my dick.

One of the airline officials motioned to us, letting us know it was safe to board the jet, so MK picked up her bag to follow Arch and Steele out onto the tarmac. My phone buzzed in my pocket as I went to follow them, and I paused to check the caller ID.

"Crap. This can't be good," I mumbled as I took the call. The airline worker indicated for me to stay off the tarmac while I was using my phone, to which I nodded my understanding.

"Roach, this is unexpected," I said as the call connected. "What's happened?"

In the background I could hear someone moaning in pain, spitting curses about something. Then came a heavy sigh directly into the speaker. "Kody, bro," the new, rather green leader of the Shadow Grove Reapers said. "You'll never fucking believe who Hades just introduced as her two new enforcers for the Timberwolves."

I stiffened. Yeah, my instincts had been right. This was not good at all. "Who?"

Roach huffed a sharp exhale. "Old man Rex is back," he told me, and I cursed. "That's not the unbelievable part, bro. The other? A goddamn fucking ghost. Cass is back, Kody. He was never dead. Cassiel fucking Saint is alive, and he's a Timberwolf now."

For a moment, I was rendered speechless. Of all the things he could have said... I'd never expected that. And yet I was relieved. Happy, even. I *liked* Cass. But...

"Fuck," I groaned. "Archer's gonna kill him."

Roach chuckled. "No shit, that's why I called you and not him. Have fun with that, bro. Catch you soon."

The line went dead, and I dragged my feet across the tarmac. Cass had been a mentor to Archer, Steele, and me since we were little kids. His "death" had been a harsh blow, but no one had taken it harder than Arch. To him, Cass was the older brother Zane had never been. He'd genuinely grieved his death... but now? Knowing he was alive and didn't say anything? Oh yeah. It was gonna be bloody.

So why did that sound like so much fun?

Maybe he'd cool down before they came to blows, though. Like MK said, it was a long flight back to Shadow Grove.

THE END

ALSO BY TATE JAMES

Madison Kate Story

(Dark NA Contemporary Romance)

#1 HATE

#2 LIAR

#3 FAKE

#4 KATE

#4.5 VAULT (novella after Hades)

HADES

(Dark NA Contemporary Romance)

#1 7th Circle

#2 Anarchy

#3 Club 22

#4 Timber

The Guild

(Dark NA Contemporary Romance)

#1 Honey Trap

#2 Dead Drop

#3 Kill Order

The Royal Trials
(Complete Fantasy series)
#1 Imposter

#2 Seeker

#3 Heir

Kit Davenport
(Complete PNR series)
#1 The Vixen's Lead

#2 The Dragon's Wing

#3 The Tiger's Ambush

#4 The Viper's Nest

#5 The Crow's Murder

#6 The Alpha's Pack

Novella: The Hellhound's Legion

Box Set: Kit Davenport: The Complete Series

Dark Legacy
(Complete Dark Contemporary high school romance)
#1 Broken Wings

#2 Broken Trust

#3 Broken Legacy

#4 Dylan (standalone)

Royals of Arbon Academy
(Complete Dark contemporary/dystopian college romance)

#1 Princess Ballot

#2 Playboy Princes

#3 Poison Throne

Hijinx Harem
(Compete RomCom PNR series)

#1 Elements of Mischief

#2 Elements of Ruin

#3 Elements of Desire

The Wild Hunt Motorcycle Club
(Dark PNR/Fantasy series)

#1 Dark Glitter

#2 Cruel Glamour (TBC)

#3 Torn Gossamer (TBC)

Foxfire Burning
(UF/PNR series)

#1 The Nine

#2 The Tail Game (TBC)

#3 TBC (TBC)

Undercover Sinners

(Dark Contemporary Suspense Romance)

Printed in Great Britain
by Amazon